"Be careful. This man has attacked you twice. Next time he might kill you."

Grace's voice shook a little at those words.

"I'm not going to let that happen."

Declan kissed her—a deep, thorough kiss she felt all the way to her toes. "I'll call you tomorrow," he said when he finally lifted his head.

"What's going to happen, with us?" She regretted the words as soon as she blurted them out. He would think she was too needy. Moving too fast.

But he didn't look upset. "We'll figure it out," he said.

She waved as he drove away. She wasn't very adept at figuring things out, but she did know a thing or two about watching and waiting.

DECEPTION AT DIXON PASS

CINDI MYERS

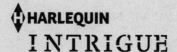

HARLEQUIN
INTRIGUE

For Dawn

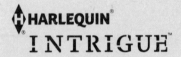

ISBN-13: 978-1-335-59037-4

Deception at Dixon Pass

Recycling programs
for this product may
not exist in your area.

Copyright © 2023 by Cynthia Myers

For questions and comments about the quality of this book,
please contact us at CustomerService@Harlequin.com.

Harlequin Enterprises ULC
22 Adelaide St. West, 41st Floor
Toronto, Ontario M5H 4E3, Canada
www.Harlequin.com

Printed in U.S.A.

Cindi Myers is the author of more than seventy-five novels. When she's not plotting new romance story lines, she enjoys skiing, gardening, cooking, crafting and daydreaming. A lover of small-town life, she lives with her husband and two spoiled dogs in the Colorado mountains.

Books by Cindi Myers

Harlequin Intrigue

Eagle Mountain: Critical Response

Deception at Dixon Pass

Eagle Mountain Search and Rescue

Eagle Mountain Cliffhanger
Canyon Kidnapping
Mountain Terror
Close Call in Colorado

Eagle Mountain: Search for Suspects

Disappearance at Dakota Ridge
Conspiracy in the Rockies
Missing at Full Moon Mine
Grizzly Creek Standoff

The Ranger Brigade: Rocky Mountain Manhunt

Investigation in Black Canyon
Mountain of Evidence
Mountain Investigation
Presumed Deadly

Eagle Mountain Murder Mystery: Winter Storm Wedding

Ice Cold Killer
Snowbound Suspicion
Cold Conspiracy
Snowblind Justice

Visit the Author Profile page at Harlequin.com.

CAST OF CHARACTERS

Grace Wilcox—The environmental scientist prefers her solitary life in a remote cabin in the mountains, continuing the research her grandfather began sixty years before. A tragedy in her past has made it hard for her to form relationships, until Declan walks out of a blizzard and into her life.

Declan Owen—The US marshal had a stellar record with the Marshal's Service until serial killer Terrence Barclay escaped his custody. Now Barclay has framed Declan for murder. Declan must clear his name and stop Barclay before he murders again.

Terrence Barclay—The serial murderer targets women in small towns. Adept at disguise, Barclay blends in with locals and has eluded Declan's attempt at apprehension.

Tommy Llewellyn—A drifter with a petty criminal record, Tommy came to Eagle Mountain for the winter and keeps trying to get Grace to go out with him. Is he really as harmless as he seems?

Mike Randolph—Mike shows up in town claiming to be the son of storeowner Arnie Cowdry's old college buddy. He, too, is attracted to Grace, and Declan senses he is hiding a lot, including his true identity.

Chapter One

Snowflakes danced in the snowmobile's head-light, swirling and corkscrewing in an elaborate ballet before adding to the already knee-high drifts on either side of the narrow path leading up to the cabin. Grace swept one gloved hand across the face shield of her helmet to clear the snow and leaned forward, squinting to try to get her bearings in this shaken–snow globe land-scape.

A dark shape lurched onto the path ahead of her, and she squeezed the brakes, the back of the snow machine fishtailing right, then left. She gasped as the headlight's blue-white glare spot-lighted the muscular image of a man, his face contorted in pain, fresh blood smeared across the side of his face, more blood on his naked chest.

All of him was naked, his skin a ghostly blue-white in the headlight's glare. Heart pounding, she braked to a stop, the snowmobile wallowing a little in the mounting drifts. "Hello!" she shouted.

The man took a step toward her, then swayed. She stood in her seat, then vaulted to the ground as he sank to his knees and toppled sideways, like a great tree felled.

He was conscious, but barely. She bent over his still form, then touched his shoulder. His skin was icy to the touch, his breathing shallow.

"Get up," she ordered, then louder, "You have to get up!" She slapped his face, and he turned away from her and moaned.

Grace shoved at his shoulders and managed to get him into a sitting position, then prodded him to his feet once more. He was a big man— over six feet tall and muscular. Snow swirled around them as she tucked her shoulder under his arm and staggered against the weight of him leaning into her.

"Come on!" she shouted over the howling wind. "We have to go."

They took one step forward, then another. Despite the exertion, her teeth chattered violently as she maneuvered him alongside her snowmobile. He didn't resist as she coaxed him onto the seat. She shrugged out of her heavy parka and draped it over him, a pitiful covering barely hanging on his broad shoulders. Then she stood behind him on the sideboard and managed to get the machine going again and headed up the path to her cabin, the single light she had left burning a beacon to guide them.

Bear, her shepherd mix, met them at the door, barking, but she quieted him. He stood back, wary, gaze flitting from her to the newcomer as she led the man to the sofa, sat him down and draped an afghan over him. He stared at her with empty, frightened eyes.

"I'm going to start a fire," she said, speaking louder than necessary, as if he was hard of hearing. She lowered her voice to a more normal tone. "We need to get you warm, then I'll help you clean up and we'll see how badly you're hurt." All that blood worried her.

She built a fire in the woodstove, and when it was blazing, she set water to heat on the gas stove in the kitchen. She grabbed the plastic basins she used for washing dishes and filled them with cool water from her storage tank and carried them to the man. "Put your hands and feet in here," she said.

When he made no move to comply, she knelt in front of him and lifted one bare foot and then the other and plunged them into one of the basins, splashing water onto the knees of her snow pants. When he tried to take them out, she pressed down. "No. Leave them in there. You'll be lucky if you don't lose toes to frostbite." His feet—large, masculine feet with fine dark hair on the toes—were so pale they were almost blue.

She looked up into his eyes, to see if he understood. He met her scrutiny, and for a moment she was caught by that gold-flecked gaze. He no longer looked so dazed.

He nodded. "Thank you," he said, his voice raspy and deep, sending a shiver along her spine.

"The second basin is for your hands." She set it on the sofa beside him.

He nodded and immersed his hands to the wrist, wincing as he did so, but he left them there.

The kettle began to sing, so Grace returned to the kitchen and made hot cocoa—a large mug with two packets of mix. She was about to add a healthy slug of brandy, then remembered the head wound and thought better of it. Instead, she poured the rest of the water from the kettle into a bowl and dug a packet of gauze and some antibiotic ointment from the first aid kit over the sink.

He was sitting where she had left him, hands and feet in the basins of water, head back and eyes closed. Bear had stationed himself by the woodstove but kept his gaze fixed on the man. Grace paused in the doorway to assess her visitor more calmly. He was probably six foot three and healthy, with well-defined muscles and good skin, a faint shadow of dark beard showing against his pale skin, well-cut dark brown hair falling across his forehead. He wore no jewelry and had no tattoos. The afghan lay across his lap, but she had a good memory of what he had looked like unclothed. Like a sleek wild animal. A little scary. A lot fascinating.

He opened his eyes and looked right at her, and heat spread up her face, as if he had known what she was thinking. "What happened?" he asked.

"I was going to ask you the same thing." She moved to his side and wet a square of gauze in the basin. The water had cooled enough now that it wouldn't burn him. She dabbed at what looked to be the source of the blood—a gash just behind his temple, jagged and already bruising at the tender edges. "I was on my way home, and you stepped out of the woods, naked and bleeding. I thought at first you were some kind of hallucination."

He grunted as she touched what must've been a tender spot. "Sorry," she said. "But this is pretty nasty. Who hit you?"

He didn't answer right away. She stopped her ministrations and tilted her head to check his expression. "I don't know," he said, his voice still ragged. "I can't remember."

The hurt in his voice touched a corresponding tender place inside of her. She had to work to catch her next breath. "It's okay," she said. "It's going to be okay." She turned her attention back to his head wound. "You might need stitches," she said. "But there's no way to get you to the medical center from here. Not in this storm."

"Where am I?" he asked.

"Officially, you're at the San Juan annex of the Rocky Mountain Biological Laboratory," she said. "Otherwise known as my house." Which, of course, made zero sense to him. Even some people who lived in Eagle Mountain didn't know about this place. That was part of its charm, both for research and personal purposes. "I collect data about weather, snowfall, rainfall, migration patterns of various species, plant growth—all kinds of things that show patterns across the years. My grandfather started the research back in 1960. It's one of the best databases of the effects of changing climate in the United States."

"You're a scientist," he said.

"Yes." So much better than other things she had been called, from *hermit* to *weirdo*. Not by her friends, of course, but some people were quick to judge. This man wasn't one of them.

"My name is Grace," she said. "Grace Wilcox." He winced as if in pain, but not physical, she didn't think. "I can't remember my name," he said, and panic tinged the last word.

She put a gentling hand on his shoulder. "It's okay," she said. "This is a nasty head wound. You might have a concussion. Your memory will probably come back to you."

Except hers never had. She had lived most of her life with a five-month gap in her recollection. Five months that had changed everything about her, yet she couldn't remember anything. She hoped this man didn't suffer that fate.

She finished cleaning the wound, dabbed on some ointment and applied a dressing. "Let me check your eyes," she said.

That direct gaze hit her again. Assessing. As if he could see all her secrets. She looked away. "Your pupils are the same size, so that's good. Any nausea?"

"A little."

"Pain?"

"Head hurts. Most of the rest of me, too."

Not a surprise, considering how far he must have walked over rough terrain. She had some ideas about that. "Do you remember anything about a car?" she asked. "A woman?" Her stomach clenched at the memory of that woman. So cold and still.

"I'm sorry," he said. "No."

She patted his shoulder again. "Let's see your hands."

The fingers were swollen now, red and painful. But she didn't think he would lose any. She dried them off, then moved to his feet. A couple of toes still showed signs of waxiness, but maybe he would be okay. If her suspicions were correct, he had been out in the weather for about an hour. Plenty of time to do damage, but not as bad as it could be.

She picked up the mug of cocoa. "Drink this," she said. "It will warm you up, and the sugar will help, too."

He couldn't really hold the mug with his swollen hands, so she held it for him while he sipped, his eyes watching her over the rim of the cup in a way she felt to the pit of her stomach. It wasn't an unpleasant feeling, but surprisingly intimate, considering she didn't even know his name.

When the mug was empty, she stood once more. "I'm going to find you some clothes." She assessed him. "They won't fit well, but they'll keep you decent."

Grace had to climb into the loft to reach the trunk with her grandfather's things. While she dug through it, she pondered her guest's possible origins. When she had found him, she had been returning from a search and rescue call up on Dixon Pass. A car had been abandoned on the side of the highway, and law enforcement had discovered a dead woman in the back seat, and a man's bloody footprints leading away from the vehicle, into the canyon. Search and Rescue had combed the area for the man responsible for those footprints but had to abandon the search after only half an hour because of the growing blizzard.

Was the man on her sofa the one who had wandered from that car? Had he killed the woman? Given his head wound, it seemed more likely to her that he had been a second intended victim and had fled for his life. It was an interesting puzzle, but one she didn't think she would know the answer to any time soon.

Near the bottom of the trunk, she found an oversized sweatshirt, a flannel shirt and a pair of sweatpants. The pants would be too short, but she added long wool socks. That would have to do. No underwear—because even she wasn't sentimental enough to have saved Granddad's Jockey shorts.

Her visitor had dozed off by the time she got back to him, but she woke him and told him sternly to dress, then left the room before he could throw off the blanket and get her heart racing again.

HE WOKE TO a crackling, popping sound and the aromas of coffee and pinion smoke. He opened his eyes and looked into the face of a woman. A beautiful woman, with dark hair falling in soft waves to her shoulders, big dark eyes framed by lacy black lashes, full pink lips and skin he ached to touch. It looked so soft.

"How are you feeling?" she asked in a gentle contralto voice.

He shook his head, not knowing how to answer. His body ached, but worse was the confusion in his mind.

She moved away and he took in the room behind her—log walls lined with bookcases, fire crackling in the woodstove and a large gray-and-black dog with a wolfish face watching him from in front of the stove.

"Your hands look better this morning," she said. "Do you think you could hold this cup of coffee?"

He looked down at his hands. They were slightly swollen and ached. He curled them into fists, then reached for the cup, even as his stomach growled.

"I'll have breakfast in a little bit," she said. "There's cream and sugar there on the table if you want them." She pointed to a small table beside him and started to turn away, but he reached out and put a hand on her arm.

"What was your name again?" He felt he should know.

"It's Grace. Grace Wilcox."

"Hello, Grace. I'm Declan Owen." Relief flooded him as he said the words. He remembered his name. That was a start.

She smiled, and he felt the warmth of her expression deep in his gut. "Do you remember what happened, Declan?"

He looked around the cabin again, then down at himself. He was dressed in too-short, too-tight sweatpants, drooping wool socks, a gray sweatshirt and a faded green-and-black flannel shirt. "I don't know how I got here," he said.

She squatted down until she was eye level with him. "What do you remember?"

He thought a moment. "I remember driving," he said. "I was following someone, I think. Or looking for someone."

"Were you alone?" she asked.

"Yes." He was certain of that. Certain that he was almost always alone.

"Were you searching for a man or a woman?" she asked.

"A man." The answer came readily.

"Anything else?" she asked.

Declan shook his head.

Grace stood. "All right. I'll make breakfast. The bathroom is right through there if you need it." She indicated a door on the far wall.

She left the room and he finished the coffee,

then went to the bathroom, which was outfitted with a composting toilet, an old-fashioned pedestal sink and a small shower. A glance out the window showed two-foot drifts with new snow falling and deep woods as far as he could see.

"The cabin is off-grid," she said when he returned to the living area. "If the snow keeps up, I'll have to go out and start the generator to recharge the batteries, but we'll be fine for a while. Breakfast is almost ready. Come into the kitchen and we'll eat there."

The kitchen was no more than an eight-foot square, with a half-size stove, refrigerator and sink and a single four-foot stretch of tiled countertop. "My grandfather built this cabin," she said. "He wasn't much of a cook and preferred to have more room for bookcases. You can sit there."

"This looks good," he said, pulling out the chair she indicated at the small table, which also looked handmade. The small space made him feel outsized, though she seemed to fit in it perfectly. "How far are we from the road?" he asked.

"There's a Forest Service road one mile down the mountain that the county plows for me, though it's not a priority." She filled a mug with fresh coffee next to a glass of orange juice, then passed a plate of bacon. "I park my Jeep at the end in winter and travel the rest of the way on a snowmobile. That's how I got you home last night."

He had brief shards of memory, like images illuminated by flashes of lightning: a woman supporting him as he tried to walk, the same woman wrapping him in a blanket. The sting of antiseptic at his temple.

He touched the bandage on the side of his head. "What happened to me?"

"It looks like someone bashed you in the head. Hard enough to knock you out, I guess." She stopped eating and laid aside her knife and fork. "I volunteer with Search and Rescue," she said. "We had a call yesterday about a car abandoned on the side of the highway up on Dixon Pass. There were a man's bloody footprints leading away from the car, and we were searching for that person. But we had to cut the search short because of the snow."

"You think the man was me?"

"Does any of that sound familiar?"

"No." He focused on his plate once more. He was famished, so much so that his hands almost shook as he spooned eggs onto his plate. They ate in silence for a while, then a new thought occurred to him. "What happened to my clothes?" he asked.

"You weren't wearing any."

He let that sink in. "Not any?"

"Not a stitch." Dimples tugged at the corners of her mouth. Was she trying not to laugh? Not exactly a thing to laugh about. "It was why I was frantic to get you inside, before you froze to death," she said.

"You made me stick my feet and hands in cold water." Why had he suddenly remembered that?

"It's supposed to allow any frozen digits to thaw, but slowly."

He looked down at his hands again. "It must have worked."

"You really should have that head looked at by a doctor," she said. "It will have to wait until the snow lets up and the plow clears the road. But I think you'll be all right until then."

"Do you have a phone?" he asked.

"I have a cell phone. And a booster so it works here. Is there someone you need to call?"

He wracked his brain but could think of no one. He shook his head. They finished eating, then he helped her clear the dishes. The kitchen was too small for them to work together, so she sent him out to the porch to retrieve more firewood. The dog, Bear, went with him and patrolled around the cabin. Declan stood for a long moment, staring at the snow falling on the silent expanse of woods. He spotted the solar panels on the roof of a nearby shed and the snowmobile parked under a lean-to beside the shed. This place was so isolated. And she lived here all alone?

Bear came up onto the porch and barked at him. "I'm not going to hurt her," Declan said softly. He knew that about himself, the way he knew his name. And then another fact popped into his head.

He went back inside and dumped his armload of wood into the old copper boiler beside the woodstove, then went to stand in the doorway to the kitchen.

Grace looked over her shoulder at him, her hands wrist-deep in soapy water. "Is something wrong?" she asked.

"I remembered something," he said. "Something important."

"Oh?"

"I'm a United States marshal. Deputy US Marshal Declan Owen."

Chapter Two

"The car is registered to Declan Owen." Sergeant Gage Walker looked up at his brother, Travis Walker, sheriff of Rayford County. Travis stood in the doorway of Gage's small office at the sheriff's department, a cup of coffee in one hand, the other braced on the door frame. Two years older than Gage, Travis was the more serious of the two, well suited to the responsibilities of sheriff. But Gage was his right-hand man, the person he counted on most to handle the toughest jobs.

"What else?" Travis took a sip of coffee and waited.

"Declan Owen is a deputy United States marshal. I tracked down his supervisor in the Denver office." He checked his notes. "Oscar Penrod. He said Owen is on vacation at the moment."

"And the woman?"

"Agnes Cockrell. She lives over in Rocky

Ridge. Her husband, Ronald, said she was driving back from visiting a friend in Purgatory."

"Driving?"

"Yeah. Her car is missing. A white Honda Element." Gage checked his notes again. "She was shot once in the back of the head with a .40-caliber bullet. We're still waiting for the ballistics tests to come back, but my guess is the bullet came from the Glock 22 found on the back floorboard near her. A gun registered to Deputy Marshal Declan Owen."

Travis let out a low whistle. "So he flags down Ms. Cockrell, shoots her and steals her car?"

"And leaves his gun behind?" Gage shook his head. "And what about those bloody footprints leading away from the car?"

"So maybe Owen was with Ms. Cockrell for some reason and a third party killed her, wounded him and he escaped."

"We might could get a frozen sample of the blood from the snow to test for blood type and DNA," Gage said.

Travis made a face. "Probably pretty diluted by snow by now, but we could try, if we have to. It would be easier to find this Declan Owen and ask him. Before tomorrow, if possible. I'd like to know what happened before I leave."

"You don't think I can handle it?" Gage asked.

Travis's look grew more pained. "I'm sure you can, but now is a terrible time for me to leave, with us being shorthanded."

"I'm not going to let you talk yourself out of taking this vacation," Gage said. "Lacy would never speak to me again. She'd probably never speak to you." Travis's wife, Lacy, had finally convinced him to take a long-delayed honeymoon to Aruba. True, the departure of Deputy Ronin Doyle, who had decided to pursue photography full time, had left them short an officer, but Gage was sure he could handle things.

"As soon as the snow lets up, we're going to ask Search and Rescue to go back out," he said. "Owen couldn't have gotten that far in that weather, bleeding the way he was."

"The blood might have belonged to Agnes," Travis said.

"I guess so."

"Anything else?" Travis prompted.

Gage consulted his notes again. "Owen spent the night at the Creekside Motel in Purgatory. His belongings are still in his room—luggage and a laptop—so it sounds like he planned to return."

"You put a BOLO out for him?"

"I did. Let's hope he turns up. Preferably alive

and not dead in the snow." Alive, they could talk to him and try to get at the truth of the situation. Dead, and they would only have more unanswered questions.

DECLAN FOUND A pair of boots by the back door that he was able to shove his feet into. He took a wedge and a splitting maul from a shelf at the end of the woodshed. He had split the first log when Grace came onto the end of the porch, a man's plaid wool shirt pulled on over her sweater and leggings. "You probably shouldn't be doing that with your head injury," she said.

"I need to do something." He brought the maul down on the wedge, and the log split with a satisfying *crack!*

She watched him a moment longer, then returned inside. He spent the rest of the morning splitting wood, until one corner of the small living area was filled with logs and his shoulders and back—and his head—ached. "Thank you," Grace said and went back to whatever she was working on at a desk in the corner of the living room.

"The snow has pretty much stopped," he said. He fed a log to the woodstove, then stood with his back to it, watching her as she studied a notebook filled with small handwriting, then typed something into a laptop. "How long before the plow makes it up this way?"

"It could be hours," she said. "Or days."

The thought of days trapped here in forced idleness grated. The idea that he needed to be somewhere, pursuing someone, gnawed at him. "Who do these clothes belong to?" Declan asked, bracing himself that the owner—her husband/boyfriend/jealous lover—would arrive shortly.

"They were my grandfather's." She held up the notebook. "This was his, too. Part of my job is to enter the data he collected for over sixty years into the lab's database. There is a lot of it, so it's taking a while." She indicated a wall of shelves behind her, which he now realized were filled with row upon row of spiral-bound notebooks.

"I'm still fuzzy on the details from last night," he said. "You're some kind of scientist?"

"That's right." She turned to face him more fully. "I spent most of my summers growing up with my grandfather, here in this cabin. I helped him collect data, which meant we spent days hiking and measuring things like how much water was in a creek and how thick the bark was on the pines and how much grass the pika were collecting for winter. I was never happier than I was when I was with him, so when it came time to go to college, I studied environmental biology. When he died two years ago, he left this cabin and all his records to me, and he also left a letter to his bosses at the lab that essentially said if they wanted the historical data he collected before he went to work for them, they needed to hire me to fill his former position."

"How did they react to that kind of demand?"

Grace laughed. "They knew my grandfather was an eccentric when they originally hired him, and old age hadn't mellowed him. I was able to show them all the proper credentials, and they were happy to hire me. It's not as if everyone wants to live up here on the side of a mountain."

"Your family doesn't worry about you up here by yourself?" he asked.

Some of the light went out of her eyes. "My grandfather was my family. And I have Bear." She ruffled the dog's head. "And I'm not a complete hermit. I volunteer with Search and Rescue and with the Colorado Avalanche Information Center, which means in winter I go out and assess avalanche conditions at various locations around Eagle Mountain and report to the center."

"You have a lot of useful skills," he said.

"And you're a marshal," she said. "What do you do, exactly?"

"The US Marshals Service is responsible for protecting federal judges and judicial witnesses," he said. "We also transport and manage prisoners, serve warrants and handle assets seized in federal cases. But I worked primarily in fugitive apprehension." The words rolled easily off his tongue, as if he had said them many times before.

"You said you were looking for someone," she said. "A fugitive?"

"I think so. I have a picture in my head, and I sense the name is almost there. More things are starting to come back to me. I hope I remember everything soon."

"Hmm." She looked as if she was going to say something, but her phone interrupted them. She picked it up from the desk beside her and checked it. "It's from Search and Rescue." She swept her thumb across the screen and read the message. "They're asking for volunteers to report to Dixon Pass to resume our search for a missing person. Oh, and they have a name now." She looked up at him. "Marshal Declan Owen."

GRACE TEXTED THAT Declan was with her, then telephoned the sheriff's department to tell them the same. The sheriff himself came on the line. "How did Deputy Marshal Owen end up with you?" Travis asked.

"I found him wandering near my cabin, disoriented and bleeding from a head injury." No need to mention his state of undress at the moment.

"How is he now?"

"Better, but he doesn't remember what happened to him. He took a pretty bad blow to the side of the head. I can bring him into town as soon as the plow clears the road up here."

"We'll come and get him," the sheriff said. "Sit tight."

The sheriff ended the call, and she laid aside the phone. "I heard most of that," Declan said. "They're coming to get me."

"I guess a fellow law enforcement officer gets first-class service," she said.

"Thanks again for everything," he said.

She looked away, pretending to tidy papers. They had only spent a few hours together, but she could admit she would miss him. It was probably the novelty of the situation. It wasn't every day that a sexy stranger ended up on her doorstep.

An hour later she heard the growl of a snowmobile climbing the hill to her house. She and Declan and Bear were on the front porch waiting when a quartet of snow machines pulled in front of the house. Sheriff Travis Walker and his brother, Sergeant Gage Walker, climbed off the first two machines, pushed up the visors of their helmets and approached.

"Deputy Marshal Owen?" Travis addressed Declan.

"Yes, sir," Owen snapped off the words with military crispness.

Travis turned to Grace. "How are you, Ms. Wilcox?"

"I'm well, Sheriff." She turned to Declan. "Marshal Owen has been a model guest."

"That's good to hear."

Gage came to stand beside Declan. "We need you to come to the station and answer some questions."

"Of course," Declan said. "Maybe you can fill me in on what happened."

Travis frowned. "What do you mean?"

"I don't remember anything from when I was driving down the highway until I woke up on Grace's sofa," he said.

"Head injuries can cause memory loss," she said.

The sheriff was still frowning. "Come with us to the station and we'll talk," he said. He turned to Grace. "We'd like you to come, too, and give us a statement."

"Of course," she said. "If you'll drop me off at my car, I'll follow you to the station. Let me get my coat."

She made sure the fire was dying down and that Bear had plenty of water, then fetched her heavy snowmobile jacket from the hook by the door. She also brought an old fleece-lined parka that had belonged to her grandfather and handed it to Declan. "You'll need this for the ride down," she said, then followed Gage to his snowmobile. The sheriff and his brother were making her uneasy, and she felt protective of Declan. Which was ridiculous. He was clearly capable of defending himself, although that hadn't been the case with whoever had attacked him.

DECLAN KNEW HE was in trouble when he saw the sheriff had brought three extra men with him. This was no courtesy ride to town. The fact that they wanted to question both him and Grace pointed to some crime having been committed—a crime beyond someone bashing him in the head and stealing his clothes.

And his gun. He was sure he'd had a gun. The thought of it missing landed a rock of dread in his stomach. He had a sense of having been in this situation before. Why couldn't he remember? Or why could he remember some things— his name, his job—and not remember why he was here or how he had ended up wandering around naked in a snowstorm?

The ride to the road was too noisy and cold in spite of his borrowed coat to make conversation possible. When they reached the forest road, Grace went to her car while Declan was ushered to a sheriff's department SUV while the two deputies were left to load the snowmobiles onto a waiting truck and trailer. Declan had plenty of questions he wanted to ask but decided to save them until he was at the sheriff's department. Instead, he looked out the window, hoping to see something familiar that would spark his memory.

Eagle Mountain proved to be a postcard-pretty community full of snowcapped Victorian buildings, tourist shops, restaurants, homes and a town park. The sheriff's department was located off the main street. Grace and Declan were led to separate interview rooms. Sergeant Walker and Sheriff Walker, apparently brothers, sat across the table from Declan and read him the Miranda notice.

"Am I being charged with a crime?" Declan asked, struggling to keep his temper in check.

"We have questions for you about the murder of Agnes Cockrell," the sheriff said.

The words landed between them like a ball of mud. Cold and ugly and feeling out of place. "Who?" Declan asked.

"Ms. Cockrell's body was found in the back

seat of your car on the side of Dixon Pass," the sheriff said. "She had been shot in the back of the head with a gun registered to you. The gun was also found in the car and yours are the only fingerprints on it."

Declan closed his eyes and groaned.

"Deputy Marshal Owen, did you shoot Ms. Agnes Cockrell?" the sheriff asked.

I don't remember, Declan thought. Could he have shot this woman whose name he didn't know?

Then a thought filled his head, icy and bracing and absolutely certain. He had been in this situation before. He knew how this worked. He sat up straighter. "No, I did not shoot Agnes Cockrell," he said. "But I think I know who did."

Chapter Three

Deputy Jake Gwynn, whom Grace knew from Search and Rescue, took down her account of how she had found Declan wandering in the snowstorm and taken him in.

"How did he get from Dixon Pass to your place?" Jake asked.

"I assume he walked," she said. "There's the hiking trail toward the falls, then an old logging road he could have followed."

"He wouldn't have been able to see the trail or the road in all that snow."

"Yes, but human instinct is to take the path of least resistance. He would have tried to steer clear of brush and trees. I think he was running for his life."

"Why do you say that?" Jake asked.

"Someone hit him in the head. And they took his clothes and shoes."

Jake frowned. "How do you know this?"

"Because he was naked when I found him. He

would have frozen to death if he hadn't come to my cabin. Maybe that was what whoever hurt him intended."

"I've heard people suffering from hypothermia will sometimes strip off all their clothes," Jake said. "Their body tricks them into thinking they're overheating."

"I've heard that, too, but I don't think that's what happened here," she said.

"What did he tell you about what happened to him?" Jake asked.

"He doesn't remember. He said he knows he was driving here, and he thinks he was looking for someone, a man. But he can't remember a name or anything that happened until he woke up on my sofa this morning."

"Do you think he's telling the truth?"

"Yes!" The word came out more insistent than she had intended. She needed to calm down. But the memory of all the people who hadn't believed her when she couldn't remember was like a hand squeezing her heart. She fought against that panicked feeling. "He's been remembering some things," she said. "He didn't know his name at first, but that's come back. And he remembered he's a US marshal."

Jake made notes on a pad. "Anything else?"

She leaned toward him. "I don't think he

killed that woman. I think whoever killed her tried to kill him, too."

"Her name is Agnes Cockrell," Jake said. "She lived over in Rocky Ridge."

"What was she doing up there in Declan's car?"

"Did you ask him?"

She shook her head. "No."

"Why not?"

Because she had been afraid to let him know about the dead woman. Just in case he was the killer. She shook her head. "It just didn't come up," she said.

"You gave him the clothes he's wearing now?" Jake asked.

"Yes. They belonged to my grandfather. They don't fit him very well, but he had to have something."

"Did he have anything else with him when you found him?" Jake asked. "Did he say anything, mention any names?"

"No. He was practically in a stupor when I found him, and very disoriented. He needs to see a doctor."

"We'll take care of that as soon as we've had a chance to talk to him."

"You can't think he did anything wrong," she said. "You should be looking for the person who attacked him and left him to die out there."

Jake gave her a curious look. "You seem pretty upset on behalf of a man you just met."

Heat burned her cheeks. He was probably thinking this was the most emotion he had ever seen her display. She knew she had a reputation of being a little standoffish. She wasn't one to get close to people. "If you had seen him out there, bleeding and half-frozen, you would feel the same," she said. Though she doubted it. The deputy looked at Declan as a murder suspect. She could only see him as someone damaged in the way she had been damaged. She had never known anyone else she shared that experience with. It felt like a gift, though one Declan probably wouldn't have wanted.

"WHO DO YOU think shot Agnes Cockrell?" Travis asked.

"His name is Terrence Barclay," Declan said. "He's a fugitive, convicted of the murder of three women in Utah, Idaho and Colorado. I was part of a detail transporting him last April for his sentencing on a fourth charge when he escaped. I think he's responsible for other murders, too."

"How did he escape?" Gage asked.

"He managed to get my gun, and he shot one of my fellow marshals and ran." Declan swallowed down the aching knot in his throat as the memories flooded back. "Later he shot another woman. With my gun."

"And you were pursuing him?" Gage asked.

Declan fisted his hands, struggling to hold his composure against a flood of anger and shame. "I was removed from the case. But then I had a tip that Barclay was headed this way. I took a vacation and decided to follow the lead."

"You were disobeying orders," Travis said.

"I was not." Not precisely. He shifted, trying to get more comfortable on the hard chair, but that was impossible. "My plan was to follow him to wherever he went to ground, then report his location to the marshals and step back and let them do their job."

"So what happened up there on the pass?" Travis asked.

"I don't know." Declan shut his eyes, but all he saw was blackness. He opened his eyes again. "There's a blank spot in my memory. I can recall before and after, but nothing up there on the pass."

Travis nodded. "Grace says you had quite a blow to the head. We'll get you to a doctor soon."

"I'm okay," Declan said. "I want to get this over with."

"You've been following this guy, Barclay," Gage said. "I assume you've studied his habits and methods. If you had to guess, what would you say happened?"

Declan took a deep breath and considered the question. This was more familiar territory, trying to guess a fugitive's next move. "He planned his kills, but he was also opportunistic. All his victims were women. Even the marshal he killed. I think maybe he came upon this woman up there. Maybe she was a hitchhiker or she had car trouble. He killed her, and maybe I interrupted him?" His head hurt. "I wish I could remember."

A knock on the door interrupted them. Gage stood and spoke to someone at the door, then sat down again. "Grace says when she found you, you were bleeding and naked. Somehow you had walked all the way from Dixon Pass."

"That's about two miles," Travis said.

"In thigh-high snowdrifts, in a storm," Gage said.

"If Grace hadn't found me, I would have died out there," Declan said. She deserved all the credit.

"Grace thinks the person who hit you took your clothes and left you to freeze to death," Gage said.

He nodded. "That sounds like something Barclay would do. He kidnapped a couple of campers once. He killed the woman, but he left the man tied to a tree in the middle of a flooded river. The water was up to the man's neck by the time someone found him."

"Why do you think Barclay was coming to Eagle Mountain?" Travis asked.

"I've got a source who said Barclay was in this area before and liked it. Then I found him registered at a motel in Purgatory under a version of one of the aliases he had used before. A man fitting his general description was using the name. By the time I checked into the same motel, Barclay had checked out, but he told the desk clerk he planned to drive to Junction."

"We should alert law enforcement in Junction," Gage said. "He could have headed there after he shot Agnes Cockrell."

"Or he's still here," Declan said.

"Why would he stay here?" Travis asked.

"I told you he likes to plan his killings. Every time before, when there's been an opportunistic murder, he's stayed in the area until he could plan and carry out a more methodical crime. He may not do that this time, but it's a pattern he's followed twice before."

"Eagle Mountain is a small community," Gage said. "Once we have his description, we should be able to spot him."

"Maybe not," Declan said. "He's very good at blending in and at establishing a false identity.

He's very average-looking to begin with, and he changes his appearance. He usually takes some kind of service job and becomes part of the community. People don't recognize him for the monster he is. We haven't been able to recognize him, either." The knowledge weighed on him.

"We'll contact the Marshals Service to get the information they can give us," Travis said.

"I should speak to my supervisor," Declan said. Penrod was not going to be pleased. After Barclay's escape, Declan had gone from one of the unit's top officers to the head of Penrod's crap list.

"I contacted him when we found your car and weapon," Gage said. "I let him know you were missing and the circumstances."

Declan nodded, though inwardly he was cringing. One more black mark against him. He could almost hear Penrod now. *How could you let this happen again?*

"That's all the questions we have for now." Travis rose. "I'll ask you to stay in town until we complete our investigation into Ms. Cockrell's shooting."

"I'd like to return to the motel in Purgatory to retrieve my belongings," Declan said. He needed his own clothes and his laptop with all the information he had amassed about Barclay.

"Of course," Travis said. "And let us know if you need help finding a place to stay."

"But first, we need to get you to the doctor," Gage said. "I'm not sure you're in good shape to drive anywhere."

He wanted to object, but he knew Gage was right. His head pounded now. And maybe a doctor knew some trick to getting his memory back.

GRACE INSISTED ON waiting for Declan. She sat on a padded chair in the small, chilly lobby, and office manager Adelaide Kinkaid brought her tea in a cardboard cup. "I guess you feel responsible for that young man, now that you saved his life," Adelaide said. Sixtysomething with a swirl of white hair and red-framed bifocals, Adelaide had a gaze sharp enough to drill through steel. She had a reputation around town as knowing everything about everybody, a powerful force for every good cause and the scourge of anyone who got out of line.

Grace blew on the tea, though it wasn't really that hot, and thought about how to answer that question. "I want to make sure he's all right," she said.

"It doesn't hurt that he's very easy on the eyes, does it?" Adelaide said and laughed.

Grace couldn't keep back a smile. There was no denying that Declan—all of him—was as close to perfect as she had had the pleasure to see. Looks weren't everything, but his were certainly nice.

The door on the left of the lobby opened, and Declan and Gage Walker emerged. Grace set aside the tea and stood. Declan seemed surprised to see her. "Is everything all right?" he asked.

"I'm fine," she said. "But I thought you might need a ride to the medical clinic."

"I can take him," Gage said. "And he'll need to get his belongings from his motel."

"I could drive you," she said.

"I thought I'd rent a car," Declan said.

"But you don't have your wallet."

He looked stumped. He turned to Gage. "Did you find my wallet in my car?"

Gage shook his head. "We didn't find your clothes, either. We combed the scene pretty thoroughly, too. And we've got your car in our lot. We're still going over it."

Declan turned back to Grace. "Thank you. I'd appreciate it if you could drive me to Purgatory to get my things."

"Doctor first," she said and took out her keys.

He followed her to her car. When they were both safely buckled in, he turned to her. "Are you okay?" he asked. "I'm guessing you've never been questioned by the police before."

"No." Not exactly. "It was okay. I know the deputy who talked to me. He's with Search and Rescue also." She put the key in the ignition but didn't start it. "I was afraid they were going to arrest you."

"Why didn't you tell me about the dead woman in my car?"

"I didn't want to upset you."

"You seem like a smart woman. You probably thought I killed her."

"I thought whoever killed her had tried to kill you." She started the engine and put the Jeep into gear.

"I think it was a man named Terrence Barclay," he said. "I've been following him. He's an escaped murderer."

The words, said in such a matter-of-fact way, still sent a chill down her spine. "You're remembering," she said.

"I remember Barclay, but I still don't remember what happened up there on the pass. I think Barclay killed Agnes Cockrell, though. I'm sorry if she was a friend of yours."

"I didn't know her," Grace said. "But it's still awful."

"It is."

They waited an hour at the clinic before he could be seen. Declan fidgeted and paced, but Grace remained calm. She'd had years to learn to sit still. It was useful for observing nature. For blending in and observing other people, too.

She'd assumed he would go back to be examined by himself, but he wasn't gone a minute before Grace was called back, to vouch for his identity and the reason for his lack of paperwork. Declan gave the number for his employer, who could provide his insurance information. He looked grim throughout the exchange, the picture of a proud man reduced to helplessness and furious about it. Grace ended up staying with him through the exam and an X-ray.

Finally, a doctor delivered a verdict. "You have a mild concussion. The amnesia you're experiencing is normal, as is the headache. You may have difficulty concentrating for the next few weeks and should limit screen time if this exacerbates your symptoms. The best treatment is rest. Don't do anything too strenuous, and try to avoid anything that could lead to another blow to the head. Your symptoms should resolve in about a month. If you're still having problems after six weeks or so, you should consult a neurologist, preferably someone with a specialty in traumatic brain injury."

Grace thought guiltily of all the firewood he had split for her that morning. That definitely qualified as strenuous activity.

"Will my memory return?" Declan asked.

"Maybe." The doctor shrugged. "Maybe not. That space of time may be a blank for the rest of your life, but you shouldn't have any permanent problems remembering other things. It may be that the cells in your brain responsible for that memory are too damaged to recover. It doesn't have any bearing on your long-term prognosis. Try not to stress over it. Stress can slow your recovery."

They dealt with the last of the paperwork and walked to Grace's car. She checked the time. It was after one. "What do you want to do now?" she asked.

"You probably have work to do," he said. "I don't want to take up more of your time."

"I set my own schedule," she said. "And I already collected the data I needed this morning." Every day she recorded the amount of snowfall on a table set up on her property for that purpose, as well as high and low temperatures, barometric pressure and other readings. It was a pattern established by her grandfather sixty-three years before. The consistency and volume of his information was one of the things that made it so valuable. "Let's drive to Purgatory and get your belongings," she said. "I'm sure you'd like to have your own clothes."

"Yes!"

She laughed at the emphatic way he spoke.

"It's not that I'm not grateful to you. And your grandfather." He looked down at his patched-together outfit. "I'm just feeling a little…exposed." It was true that the tight sweatpants clung to his backside and thighs in a distracting way. Distracting for her, at least.

"Then let's get you something more comfortable."

Grace hadn't even realized she had slowed the Jeep as they neared the top of Dixon Pass until he asked, "Is this where they found my car?"

"Yes." She pressed down on the accelerator, thinking she would speed past.

"Stop," he said. "Please. Maybe something here will trigger my memory."

She did as he asked, pulling over on the patch of packed-down snow where emergency vehicles must have parked. They both got out, and she led the way to the edge where his car had been. Fresh snow had dressed the scene in white, theirs the only footsteps on the surface, though she could see the ruts and ridges where others had walked and parked the morning before.

Declan stood, hands in the deep pockets of her grandfather's old jacket, and stared into the valley below. "I was down there?" he asked.

She moved to stand beside him. "There's a trail down from here." She pointed to a path along a narrow ledge that followed a series of switchbacks down. "It's the only way you could have traveled from here. There were bloody footprints leading down there. We followed them as far as that clump of trees." She pointed to a stop a quarter mile down the trail. "Then the snow got too heavy. It wasn't safe to keep looking."

"How did I manage to stay on the trail in a snowstorm?" he asked. "I couldn't have known where I was going."

"You have good survival instincts," she said. She had heard plenty of stories from fellow rescue volunteers about impossible situations where people shouldn't have lived but had.

Declan stared for a long while, then turned away. "I'm not remembering anything."

They returned to the Jeep and set out again. "What happens if I never remember?" he asked.

"You'll get on with your life," she said. "It might not be easy, but you'll do it, because you can't do anything else."

"You sound so sure." He shifted to turn toward her. "How do you know?"

She swallowed. She didn't talk about this with anyone. But he needed to hear. To know he wasn't alone. She would have given anything to have that comfort. "When I was nine years old, I was injured in a car accident. I don't remember anything for two months before the accident or three months after. Five months of my life are a total blank. They probably always will be."

"You don't remember anything?" he asked.

She shook her head. "Only what people have told me." What her mother had told her, the words full of so much anger and pain. Anger and pain Grace carried inside her.

"I'm sorry," he said. "I guess I'm lucky to have only lost a day."

"It's still a loss."

He didn't say anything for a long moment. She stared out the windshield, mechanically guiding the car through a landscape of towering cliffs and icy waterfalls that most times left her in awe. All she felt now was the familiar numbness that she pulled around her like a shield.

Then Declan reached over and took her hand. She felt the strength of him in spite of his gentleness, and a warmth that seeped into her, thawing places that had been frozen for as long as she could remember.

Chapter Four

"What do you think?" Gage settled into the chair in the sheriff's department and studied his brother. Travis would have an opinion about Declan Owen, though he rarely volunteered anything, even to Gage.

"We'll have to see how much of his story checks out." Travis drummed his fingers on his desk. "Ask Ronald Cockrell if he or his wife knew Owen or Grace Wilcox."

"Grace?" Gage felt the tension in the back of his neck. "You think she's tied up in this?"

"Do you think Owen made it all the way from Dixon Pass to her place, naked and bleeding, in a blizzard?" Travis asked.

"I don't know," Gage said. "People do all kinds of seemingly impossible things. Last year there was a guy who climbed Everest, by himself, with no supplemental oxygen. In winter."

Travis shook his head. "Maybe. What do you know about Grace Wilcox?"

Gage thought for a moment, gathering what he knew about the quiet brunette. "She's one of the new trainees with Search and Rescue. I've seen her on a few calls. She's some kind of researcher or something—lives in that cabin up past Forest Service Road 617." He shrugged. "That's about it."

"She works for the Rocky Mountain Biological Lab," Travis said. "She took over the position from her grandfather. That's his cabin she's living in. I guess she inherited it along with the job. She moved here from Iowa after he died last year."

Gage didn't ask how Travis knew this. Big brother prided himself on knowing about every one of his constituents in this small county. "I don't see the connection to Owen," he said. "He's from Denver."

"They struck me as pretty close for two people who just met," Travis said.

"If she really found him the way she said she did, she saved his life, taking him into her cabin," Gage said. "Maybe she feels responsible."

"Maybe."

"Do you think Owen is telling the truth when he says he can't remember what happened to him?" Gage asked.

"I've heard head trauma can cause temporary

amnesia," Travis said. "But there's no way to prove that. There's one thing that bothers me about his story, though."

"If he was following Barclay, where's Barclay's car?" Gage asked. "And where's Agnes Cockrell's car?"

Travis nodded. "Let's say Barclay did kill Cockrell, put her in Owen's car and hit Owen in the head, stole his clothes and abandoned him to freeze to death. He leaves Owen's car and drives away in either his own or Cockrell's car. That still leaves one vehicle unaccounted for."

"What do you think happened?" Gage asked.

"I don't know. Maybe Barclay and Owen were together. Maybe Owen stopped to help Cockrell and Barclay took advantage of the situation."

"Owen is supposed to be on vacation," Gage pointed out.

"He's already admitted he was using that time to track Barclay."

"I guess if a felon had taken my weapon and used it to kill a fellow officer, I'd want to track him down, too," Gage said.

Travis sent Gage a sour look. Of course big brother would never step out of line that way, but Gage had sympathy for Owen—if what he had told them was true.

Gage pulled out his phone. "I'll get the official records from the Marshals Service, but in the meantime…" He pulled up a browser and typed in *Terrence Barclay*. He scanned the search results, then sat up straighter. "Here we go." He read from the news story he had found. "Convicted murderer Terrence Barclay escaped custody today. Barclay was being transported to Larimer County Courthouse to stand trial for the murder of Alice Faye Cumberland when he overpowered one of the federal marshals escorting him, then used that marshal's gun to kill a female marshal." He looked up from the screen. "So that part of Owen's story checks out."

"See if you can get more details from the Marshals Service," Travis said. "And I'd be interested in knowing where they think Barclay is headed."

Gage tucked the phone away and stood. "I'll get on it."

Adelaide leaned into the office. "We just had a call from dispatch. Some climbers found a wrecked car over in Carson Canyon."

"That's not far from Dixon Pass." Travis shoved back his chair and stood.

"Maybe it's one of the missing vehicles we're looking for," Gage said.

Adelaide consulted the slip of paper in her hand. "The climbers who called it in didn't see any sign of a driver, but they did note the license plate number. It's registered to an Angela Jimenez in Purgatory."

"And?" Gage prompted. The knowing look in Adelaide's eye told him there was more.

"And Ms. Jimenez reported the car stolen yesterday morning."

"We'll need to send Search and Rescue down there to check for anyone in the vehicle or someone who might have been ejected when the car went over," Travis said.

"I'm betting we don't find anyone," Gage said.

"Does this have anything to do with that US marshal you were questioning earlier?" Adelaide said. "Or Grace Wilcox?"

"What do you know about Ms. Wilcox?" Travis asked.

Gage wished he had thought to ask the question first. Adelaide made it her business to find out everything she could about everyone in town. It was one of her finer qualities—and a source of irritation, since no one kept secrets for long from Addie.

"She used to come here every summer as a child to stay with her grandfather, Hugh Wilcox, up in that cabin near Wilson Peak," Adelaide said. "I would have said that old hermit had about as much business taking care of a little girl as a bear, but she seemed to take to running half-wild in the woods all summer. I hadn't seen her around for a few years when she came back to settle his affairs, and then she ended up staying on. She moved into the cabin and took up his old position with the research lab. I was half-afraid she would turn into a hermit like him—a pure waste—but she seems to be making an effort lately to get involved. She volunteered with the Avalanche Information Center, adopted a dog from the animal shelter and joined up with Search and Rescue."

"You sound like you like her, Addie," Gage teased.

She fixed him with a gaze that automatically made him want to stand up straighter and apologize for whatever he had done wrong. "I admire people who do good work and don't complain. Grace is like that. I worried about her being lonely up there in that remote cabin with just a dog for company, but now she's turned up with just about the handsomest man to show up around here in a long time. So I guess I admire that, too."

Gage worked to suppress his laugh. Men of all ages and stripes had been left speechless by Addie's not-so-subtle flirting, though he suspected she enjoyed the game more for her ability to unsettle the opposite sex, since she remained steadfast to the memory of her late husband.

"Thanks, Addie," Travis said.

"Grace isn't in any trouble, is she?" Adelaide asked.

"Not sure." Travis moved past her. "But if she is, I expect you'll find out before we do."

DECLAN'S HEAD THROBBED, and the bright sun streaming through the windshield of Grace's Jeep made his vision blur. He closed his eyes and leaned his head against the passenger window for the rest of the drive to the motel. Why could he remember some things—like the number and location of his motel room—but not what had happened up there on the pass? Not knowing what Barclay might have done—and what he himself had failed to do—clawed at him like briars under his skin. After Barclay had taken his gun the first time, Declan had sworn that would never happen again. He would never let his guard down that way. That failure in his duty still haunted him.

And yet he had ended up stripped of everything, including his weapon, and Barclay must have been responsible. If only he could remember.

"Is this the place?"

Grace's question brought him back to the present. Declan opened his eyes and looked at the sign for the Miner's Rest Inn. "This is it," he said. "My room is around back."

"We'll need to get the key from the front desk," she said.

Right. Because he had nothing. Not even his room key.

The clerk on duty was the same young woman who had checked him in two mornings ago—Kimberley, her name tag identified her. She smiled as he stepped in the door. "Mr. Owen! I was getting a little worried about you. House-keeping said they didn't think you'd been back to your room since yesterday morning."

"I got delayed." He looked down at his mis-matched clothing. "Actually, I was in an accident."

"Oh no!" She put a hand to her mouth, then her gaze shifted up to the bandage at his temple. "What happened?"

He opened his mouth to make up some story, but his brain refused to come up with anything. Grace stepped forward to rescue him. "He was in a car wreck," she said. "He ended up losing everything, including his wallet and his room key. But I'm sure you have his information on file from when he checked in?"

"Oh, sure," Kimberley said. "And we can get you a new key."

"Thanks," he said, including both women in

the sentiment. "I just need to change clothes, then I'll be checking out."

"No problem." Kimberley programmed a new key card and handed it over. "I'm so sorry about your accident. I hope everything is okay."

"It will be," he said, hoping that statement was true.

They returned to Grace's Jeep, and she drove him around back to his room. Relief flooded him when he saw nothing in the room had been disturbed. His laptop was still locked in the case in the closet, his clothes hanging on the rod above.

"Is everything okay?" she asked.

He nodded. "I'll change in the bathroom, and then we can go."

"Don't rush on my account." She sat in a chair by the window and pulled out her phone.

One look in the bathroom mirror made him groan. His right eye was swollen, the white bandage at his temple was stained with a little dried blood, as was his hair, which needed a trim and combing. His beard was coming in heavy along his jaw. He wanted a shower but settled for wetting down his hair and combing out as much of the blood as possible, and shaving. Then he changed into jeans and a fleece pullover, put on the running shoes he found in the closet next to his suitcase, then folded the borrowed clothing and tucked it in the plastic bag meant for laundry.

"I can't thank you enough," he said when he handed the bag to Grace.

"I'm happy to do it," she said.

"You even sound like you mean it."

Her lips curved into a smile, and the heat behind the look hit him in the gut. "My normal life is pretty boring. It's nice to have something to shake things up."

That was one way to put it. "No daring rescues in the mountains?" he teased.

She shook her head. "I've only been with the group a few months." She stood. "Are you ready to go?"

He picked up his suitcase and computer bag. "I need a phone," he said. "And I need my credit cards and a driver's license before I can get the phone."

"You can borrow mine to call the credit card companies." She pulled the phone from her pocket. "Do you remember what cards you had?"

"I have a file on my computer with that information."

"That's very organized of you."

"My dad was a general in the Army. He drilled organization and being prepared for anything into me and my sister."

She nodded and opened the door. He followed her to the Jeep and stowed his luggage in the back. When he joined her in the front again, she was staring at her phone. "I just got a text from Search and Rescue," she said. "They need people to search for survivors of a wreck in Carson Canyon. Apparently a car went off the road." She started typing. "I'm letting them know I'm in Purgatory and won't be able to make it."

"I'm sorry," he said. "I'm keeping you from things you need to do."

"It's all right." She tucked the phone away again. "Not everyone can make every call. And I'm still a rookie. I'm not going to be the person they send into a canyon. I'm still training on climbing and canyon descents and things like that."

"I'm impressed," he said. "I'm not sure I'd want to do that."

"I'm sure as a marshal you're used to doing dangerous things." She pulled out of the motel lot, back onto the highway.

"I doubt I can get my credit cards reissued before a couple of days," he said. "In the meantime I'm going to need somewhere to stay." He glanced at her. "I'm not asking you to take me in. You've done enough." And it would be easier for him to keep tabs on the sheriff's department's investigation if he was staying somewhere less remote.

"I have a friend in Search and Rescue," she said. "Her parents own an inn in town. I think they'll put you up. I'm sure the sheriff will vouch for you."

He wasn't so sure of that. To Sheriff Walker, he was still a murder suspect. Nothing personal—that was just where the evidence pointed. And Declan hadn't been able to say much to defend himself. *I can't remember* could sound like a convenient excuse to someone who wasn't sitting where he was sitting.

"The canyon where that vehicle is isn't very far from Dixon Pass," Grace said. "Do you think the car they found might belong to the man you're looking for?"

The hair on the back of his neck stood up. He shifted toward her. "Why do you say that?"

"I was just wondering. If he was there and the woman who was killed was there and they both had vehicles, he could have driven away in one car, but what happened to the other one?"

"Can I borrow your phone?" he asked her.

"Of course." She pulled the phone from her pocket and handed it over again. He searched and found the number for the Rayford County Sheriff's Department and asked to speak to Travis Walker. "I'm with Grace in Purgatory," he said. "We just picked up my things from the motel, and Grace got a text from Search and Rescue about a vehicle in a canyon."

"The car belongs to Angela Jimenez," Walker said. "Do you know her?"

"No. But Barclay has stolen cars before."

"You said you were following him yesterday," Travis said. "If he stole a car, why not report that?"

"I don't know," he admitted. A stolen car would have been the perfect excuse to stop Barclay and hold him. "Unless I didn't know the car was stolen." Had he missed that, too? Or had Barclay obscured the plate or been far enough ahead of Declan that he hadn't been able to read the license? What had really happened? "You should check the vehicle for Barclay's prints."

"You don't have to tell us how to do our job," Walker said.

"Of course not."

"Do you know yet where you're going to be staying in Eagle Mountain?" Walker asked. "How we can get in touch with you?"

"Grace is taking me to a place owned by friends of hers."

"The Alpiner," she interjected.

"The Alpiner," he repeated. "I'm going to contact my credit card company and get them to reissue my cards and cancel my old ones, then purchase a new phone. I'll give you the number when I have it."

"Do that," Walker said.

"Will you let me know what you find out?" he asked, trying not to sound like he was begging. "With this car and with Agnes Cockrell's murder?"

"You're supposed to be on vacation," Walker said.

The call ended before he could think of a suitable answer. He stared at the phone. "The call dropped," he said.

"It's hard to keep a signal here in the mountains," she said. "You can try again when we get back to Eagle Mountain."

He didn't bother telling her he wasn't going to waste any more time with the sheriff. Like his bosses, Travis Walker would tell him this was none of his concern.

But their reputations weren't on the line like his was. And right now, Terrence Barclay was at the top of the US Marshals' priority list. If Declan could track him down, he had a chance at redeeming himself.

Chapter Five

Declan wore his frustration in the hunch of his shoulders and the furrow of his brow. Grace wanted to reach out and smooth those lines of pain away, to erase the fear she suspected was at the base of his barely contained anger. *What happens if I never remember?* The plaintive note in his voice when he had asked the question still burned her.

You'll live, she wanted to tell him. *But part of you will always be missing.* He wouldn't want to hear that. A man like him wouldn't want to accept that there was something—especially something about himself—that he couldn't fix.

"Maybe this Barclay you've been hunting died when his car went into that canyon," she said. Not that she wished anyone's death, but would knowing his quarry was no longer on the loose give him any peace?

"That car is in the canyon because Barclay put it there," he said.

"Why?"

"To buy time. He's left a string of stolen vehicles behind over the years. Barclay used a stolen vehicle in connection with every murder he committed. He'll end up ditching Agnes Cockrell's car, too, as soon as he thinks it's a liability."

"Have you been following him for a long time?" she asked.

"Five years," he said. "I was part of the team that tracked him down after his fourth murder. Larimer County was getting ready to try him for that one when he escaped."

"Where do you think he is now?"

He blew out a breath. "My best guess is that he's in Eagle Mountain." He glanced at her. "I'm not trying to frighten you, but it's what he's done before. After every spontaneous killing, like the murder of Agnes Cockrell, he's picked out another victim and stalked her. It's as if he has a need to carry out a meticulously planned crime, one where he thinks he can control all the variables. It may sound strange, but he doesn't really like risk, for all the risky things he's done."

"He could have killed you," Grace said, her mouth dry at the knowledge.

"I don't know why, but he doesn't kill men."

"I don't think I could do what you do," she said.

"I imagine there's less violence in nature," he said. "At least, malicious violence."

"Yes." There was sadness and death in nature, and the story the data she collected told about the changing climate could be frightening. But there was no hatred behind the facts and figures, and no personal threat to herself, at least not in the short term.

She drove to the Alpiner and led the way inside. Brit Richards looked up from behind the front desk. "Hello, Grace." She glanced past her to Declan, her expressive face not hiding her curiosity. "What can I do for you?"

"This is Marshal Declan Owen," she said. "Declan, this is Brit Richards. Her daughter, Hannah, is a local paramedic and one of the search and rescue volunteers I work with."

"Deputy Marshal Owen," he corrected and offered his hand. "It's nice to meet you, Ms. Richards."

"Call me Brit. Everyone does. How can I help?"

"I need a place to stay for a few days," he said. "But I was in an accident and lost my wallet with all my credit cards. I'm going to contact my bank today about reissuing them, and I'll get the information to you as soon as I can."

"The sheriff can confirm his identity if you need him to," Grace said.

"Oh, that won't be necessary." Brit turned to her computer terminal. "We've got a single on the second floor available, if that's all right," she said. "It includes breakfast."

"That would be great," he said. "I really appreciate it."

While he was completing the registration, the front door opened and Hannah entered, accompanied by her fiancé, Deputy Jake Gwynn. "Hey, Grace," Hannah said. "We missed you on the accident call. Sheri said you were in Purgatory." She cast a curious glance at Declan.

"Hello, Grace," Jake said. "Marshal Owen."

"Did you find anyone at the accident site?" Declan asked.

Hannah sent another questioning look to Grace, but before she could explain, Jake said, "Nobody was there. We think whoever was driving the car may have sent it into that canyon on purpose."

"Why would someone do something like that?" Brit asked.

"For the insurance money," Jake said. "To hide evidence. There are all kinds of reasons."

The muscles bunched along Declan's jaw, as if he was clenching his teeth to keep from saying something.

"I hear you think you know who was driving that car," Jake said.

Declan nodded. "His name is Terrence Barclay. He has a habit of stealing vehicles, then ditching them."

Jake nodded. "It's going to take a couple of days to get the vehicle out of the canyon. When we do, we'll go over it."

"You won't find anything," Declan said. "Barclay doesn't leave much behind."

"Nothing turned up on your car," Jake said. He opened his mouth as if to add more, then glanced at Brit and shut it again.

"How long will you be staying with us, Marshal?" Hannah asked. She moved behind the counter to join her mother.

"I'm not sure," he said. "Is that a problem?"

"Not at all," Brit said. "It's not our busy time of year."

"I may want to talk to you later," Jake said. "I'd like to know more about Barclay." He sounded friendly enough that some of the tension went out of Declan's shoulders.

"Sure," he said. "I'm happy to tell you what I know."

"Jake and I are meeting with Lena Griffith in a bit," Hannah told her mom. "She has some new properties to show us." She turned to

Grace. "Jake and I are trying to find a house, but the market isn't very friendly right now."

"If you keep looking, something will turn up," Brit said. She handed Declan a key card. "The stairs are behind you, or head left at the end of the corridor and there's an elevator."

"The stairs are fine." Hannah and Jake said goodbye and left, and Brit disappeared into an office behind the front desk.

Declan turned to Grace. "Thank you again for everything," he said.

She plucked a business card from a holder on the counter and wrote down her name and number, then pressed it into his hand. "Call me if you need anything," she said. "A ride or a loan or…anything."

"You've done enough already," he said and tucked the card into the pocket of his jeans.

"I want to help," she said. *I don't want to lose track of you yet.*

"I'd better go." She left before she said or did something foolish. Of course, he would leave. He would go back to his job and his home, and she would never know what happened to him. That was how things worked. She ought to be used to that by now.

DECLAN SAT ON the side of the bed in his room at the Alpiner Inn and stared at the phone on the table beside him. He needed to call his bank and his cell phone provider, credit card issuers. But first he had to contact his boss. Oscar Penrod would have heard from the Rayford County Sheriff's Department by now and had probably been lighting up Declan's cell phone—wherever it happened to be.

He squared his shoulders and picked up the handset.

"Marshal Penrod's office."

"Hello, Carlos. This is Declan. I need to speak to Marshal Penrod."

Silence. The kind that held weight. "The marshal has been expecting your call. For some time."

Carlos wasn't the only one who knew how to use a pause to his advantage. Declan said nothing.

"One moment," Carlos finally said, an extra crispness to his voice. Seconds later, Declan's supervisor was on the line.

"Deputy Marshal Owen, would you care to explain to me why a county sheriff from a place I've never heard of called to tell me first that you were missing altogether, then to tell me you had been found but were a suspect in a murder investigation?"

Declan winced and rubbed his uninjured temple. "I didn't kill anyone," he said. At least, he was pretty sure he hadn't.

"This Sheriff Walker tells me a woman was shot with your gun, her body found in the back seat of your car and yours were the only prints on the gun."

"Did he also mention someone—probably the killer—knocked me unconscious and left me for dead in the middle of a blizzard? I didn't shoot that woman—who I don't know—and then do that to myself."

Penrod grunted. "Walker also wanted to know about Terrence Barclay. He told me you claim to have been tracking Barclay, and the next thing you knew, you woke up in a strange cabin miles from your vehicle. I thought it was one of the wildest stories I'd ever heard. What is he leaving out?"

"I don't remember what happened," Declan said. "Not yet. The doctor said the head injury messed with my memory."

"But you admit you were tracking Barclay? That's not your case. And you're supposed to be on vacation."

"I had a credible tip that Barclay was in the area. I decided to follow him—discreetly—to see where he was going and report his location to you."

"Oh, you did? You obviously didn't follow

discreetly enough, if he's the one who cold-cocked you and used your weapon to murder a woman. I have never in my history with the US Marshals Service had an officer who was overcome by fugitives twice. Guarding your sidearm is policing 101."

"Yes, sir." Even though he was alone, Declan's face burned. "I don't know how it happened. I wasn't careless."

"You lost your weapon and your man. If that isn't careless, I don't know what is."

"Yes, sir." He held his breath, counting to ten before he trusted himself to say more. What he had to say next was really going to send Penrod over the top. "Barclay took my badge and credentials, too. I'll need replacements."

Silence. The kind of silence that drilled a hole in Declan's stomach. "Sir?" Declan said when he could stand it no longer.

"You don't need your credentials," Penrod said. "As of this moment you are on indefinite leave."

His heart plummeted. Were they sacking him? Just like that? "Sir?"

"You've had a head injury. You're on medical leave until a physician clears you to return to work. You're also on administrative leave pending the resolution of this murder investigation and our own internal investigation as to what happened. Expect to hear from our investigators."

"Yes, sir." The reply was automatic, drilled into him by his father long before the Marshals Service had reinforced the response.

"Goodbye," Penrod said and hung up.

Declan lay back on the bed and closed his eyes. He was in up to his neck this time. He'd be lucky to keep his job after this, let alone any self-respect.

He shifted and felt something in his pocket. He pulled out the card Grace had given him and studied the precise printing—like an architect's handwriting. Or a scientist used to recording accurate data in logbooks in the field to be transcribed at a later date.

He would have bet that nine out of ten women would have run screaming when he'd come staggering out of that blizzard toward her. Why hadn't she? She was the only one here who didn't look at him skeptically when he said he couldn't remember what had happened to him up on Dixon Pass. Was it because of her own experience with memory loss or an extra measure of compassion or some other quality he couldn't identify?

He propped the card on the bedside table and lay back again. He had given Grace enough trouble already, so he should do her a favor and throw that card away.

But he wouldn't do so. He was really out on his own this time, and he wasn't going to be foolish enough to turn away from a friend if he got desperate.

Chapter Six

Saturday morning, Gage stood in the mud and gravel of the wrecker service storage yard in Delta and stared at the white Honda Element with a faded Coexist sticker on the left side of the bumper. A car registered to Agnes Cockrell. "We hauled it out of a no-parking zone in the alley behind a bakery, over off Sixth Avenue," the wrecking yard owner—a compact, wiry man with a bushy black beard—told him. "Yesterday. No plates, but when we ran the VIN, we saw it had been reported stolen, then saw the note to contact the Rayford County Sheriff's Department."

"Thanks," Gage said. "I'll get someone over this afternoon to take it to our impound lot." An evidence team would go over the car thoroughly. If they were lucky, they might get a print or some fibers, but he wasn't holding his breath. The car stolen from Angela Jimenez hadn't turned up any evidence. Apparently, Terrence Barclay was very careful. And very lucky.

"Somebody commit a crime in that car?" the bearded guy asked.

"Something like that." Gage moved closer and peered into the vehicle. A woman's purse lay on its side in the passenger well—tissues, a wallet and various pieces of paper spilling out of it. Next to that, pieces of broken plastic and glass. Gage squinted to bring the items into sharper focus and realized he was looking at a smashed cell phone. Agnes Cockrell's or Declan Owen's?

Owen had a new phone now. Gage had seen him talking on it, standing in front of the Alpiner Inn when Gage had driven past on his way to Delta. Gage had kept track of Owen the last couple of days, without appearing to do so, in between his extra duties now that Travis was on vacation. The marshal had kept a low profile. He had rented a vehicle, so he must've gotten his credit card situation figured out, though Gage had to wonder if he had been cleared to drive.

Gage hadn't seen any sign of Grace Wilcox these past two days. Had Owen persuaded her that he didn't need her anymore? Gage had been struck by how attached Grace had been to Owen, despite her reputation of being almost as reclusive as her grandfather had been.

Maybe later he would head up to Grace's cabin and ask her again about the rescue call and her first encounter with the injured Declan Owen. He wanted to see if anything about her story had changed or if she remembered anything Owen had said that might clear up the mystery of what, exactly, had happened up on Dixon Pass that day.

Gage drove back to Eagle Mountain, his mind turning over the bits of information he had collected so far, trying to make them fit together into a clear picture. But he didn't have enough yet to come to any conclusions. Owen might've had the answers he needed, but the marshal either wasn't able or wasn't willing to tell what he knew.

Gage pulled into his parking spot behind the sheriff's department and started toward the back door but stopped short when a figure stepped from the shadows to the left of the door.

"It's just me, Sergeant."

Owen looked better today, in clothes that fit, freshly shaved and his hair trimmed. The bandage on his temple was gone, the bruise still swollen and mottled purple and yellow. "What can I do for you, Marshal?" Gage asked.

Owen met his gaze firmly, almost angrily. "I need to talk to you and the sheriff about Terrence Barclay," he said.

"What about him?" Gage asked.

"There are things you need to know about him. Things I know because I've been following him for so long."

"I've read the reports the Marshals Service sent over," Gage said.

"Not everything is in those reports."

Why not? Gage wondered. But he thought he knew. Reports were full of facts. Numbers, dates and other things that could be easily measured. But part of police work was based on instinct and gut feelings and educated guesses. These were the sort of things that had no place in official reports or in courts of law. You didn't base an arrest on those non-tangibles, but you didn't ignore them, either. Sometimes they made the difference between finding the person responsible for a crime and having a case grow ice-cold.

"Let's go inside and talk," he said and unlocked the door. He would listen to what Owen had to say, then decide if he believed him.

SATURDAY MORNING, Grace attended a training class at Search and Rescue headquarters. All of the new recruits were required to attend, with veterans there to assist. She took her turn practicing the knots SAR Captain Sheri Stevens demonstrated—knots they would use to secure lines to equipment to be lowered down a steep slope or into a canyon, knots to fasten a litter to an overhead line, knots they might use when climbing themselves. Grace wouldn't win any prizes for speed, but she had a good memory and was able to complete each knot perfectly.

"That's great, Grace," Sheri said. "I want you to practice those every day until you're able to tie each one in under thirty seconds, preferably in pitch dark."

"Even better if you stand in a freezer while you do them," Hannah Richards, who was helping Sheri with the class, said. "And aim a fan, turned up on high, so that it blows ice pellets sideways at you while you do it."

"You make it sound like so much fun," Grace said but smiled so they knew she was teasing. She didn't have the easy banter these two did, but she was trying.

"Don't let us scare you off," Sheri said. "You're doing great. Much better than Hannah did when she first started."

"Me!" Hannah pretended outrage. "What about you?"

"I was already a competitive climber when I joined SAR," Sheri said. "One thing I knew how to do was tie knots."

"But you couldn't place a splint correctly for the longest time." Hannah nudged Grace. "Everyone has their strengths and weaknesses," she said. "It's one of the great things about SAR. Everyone brings something to the team."

Grace didn't point out that she wasn't a climber or a paramedic, but she understood what Hannah was trying to say. "I'm glad to be a part of the organization," she said. "I'm looking forward to having the skills to be able to contribute more."

"You contribute a lot already," Sheri said. "You're calm under pressure, you have a good memory and you follow directions well. And you aren't afraid of tough situations. Those are all the perfect qualities for working search and rescue."

"I hear you already saved at least one life," Hannah said. At Grace's blank look, she laughed. "Don't tell me you've already forgotten a certain good-looking US marshal."

Heat flooded Grace's cheeks, and she stared at the knotted ropes in front of her.

"Is it true he was naked when you found him?" Sheri asked.

Grace nodded. "I'm amazed he hadn't already frozen to death out there in that storm."

"He seems plenty healthy now," Hannah said. "Yesterday morning, I bumped into him coming out of the little gym we have at the inn. I know

I'm an engaged woman, but *Mama*! He is one very nicely put-together man."

"Yes. He is," Grace agreed and couldn't keep back a smile.

"How long is he going to be in town?" Sheri asked. She began coiling up the ropes. Around them, others were doing the same.

"He's not sure." Sheri seemed to assume that she and Declan were in touch. Grace didn't want to admit she hadn't seen or even talked to him in two days. She told herself he was probably busy, but she couldn't deny her hurt. Of course Declan didn't owe her anything, but she had thought they'd had a connection. Guess he hadn't felt it.

Class ended and she said goodbye to the others and headed into Eagle Mountain to run some errands. The trek from her cabin was difficult enough that she tried to get as much done as possible when she ventured out. She collected mail from her box at the post office, returned a library book and checked out another, picked up dog food at the pet store, then decided to get a few groceries.

The strap of sleigh bells on the door of the natural foods store jangled loudly as she entered, and a young man in a green apron, brown hair cut short in back and long on top, looked up. "Hey," he said and grinned. He had an open, friendly face with ruddy cheeks and freckles across his nose.

"Oh, hello." She looked around. "Where's Arnie?" The older man who owned the store was usually behind the counter.

"He ran into Junction to pick up a new order," the man said. "I'm Mike. I just started. What can I do for you?"

"I just need a few things. I'll help myself." She headed for the bulk bins along the side wall, aware of him watching her.

"Do you like tea?" he asked after a moment.

She paused in the act of scooping steel-cut oats into a paper bag. "I do," she said.

"We have some great chai Arnie's getting from a new supplier." He came out from behind the counter and moved to her side, tea tin in hand. "It's really spicy. Lots of flavor." He took the lid from the tin and held it out to her. The aromas of cinnamon and cardamom filled the air.

"I'll try some," she said. "A small bag."

"I'll measure that out for you." He stepped back, and she relaxed a little. He had a nice smile and a friendly manner. There was no reason for her to be nervous.

She completed her shopping and carried her items to the counter. Mike handed her the bag of tea. "Let me know what you think," he said.

"Uh, sure."

He chuckled. "Not that Arnie trusts me to tell him what to stock, but it would give me an excuse to talk to you again."

She returned the smile. "I guess if you're new in town, you don't know many people yet."

"You would be right. But as you can see, I'm trying. You can be one of my first friends, Miss…?"

"Wilcox. Grace Wilcox."

"It's good to meet you, Grace." He took her hand. "I hope I'll be seeing a lot more of you."

Grace marveled at the exchange as she stowed her groceries in her Jeep, then drove to the gas station. She had never been the type to make friends easily and had to work to put herself out there, even in a place as friendly as Eagle Mountain. Joining Search and Rescue was helping her get to know more people, but she was still skilled at melting into the background. People—men—just didn't notice her. Maybe Mike was simply the type to go out of his way to make friends with everyone. It wasn't as if he'd been flirting with her. Had he?

She passed the Alpiner on the way to the gas station and hit the brakes momentarily. She should go in and see if Declan was there. She could say she wanted to check on him. Or invite him to dinner?

She removed her foot from the brake and ac- celerated forward. If Declan wanted to see her, he had her number and he knew where she lived.

At the gas station, she pulled up to the pump and got out of the car. Next to her, a big red van idled. The driver, a young man with an orange knit hat pulled down over his ears, came around to the pump. "Hey," he said and nodded to her.

She nodded in return and slid her credit card into the reader at the pump.

"Do you live around here?" the man in the hat asked.

"Near here," she hedged.

"Sorry. I didn't mean to make you nervous." He offered a shy smile. "I just got into town, and I wondered if you knew of any campgrounds around here. Or free places to park my van and stay a few days."

She shook her head. "Sorry. I don't know. Maybe...the visitor's center? Or the library?"

"That's a great idea. They can probably help me out." He took the nozzle from the pump. "Maybe I'll see you around again." He turned to fill his van.

Grace completed her own transaction and drove away in a daze. She could count on the fingers of one hand the number of times two good-looking young men had sought out a con- versation with her in one day. She had made a lifetime habit of keeping herself apart from other people, and most of them picked up on her *leave me alone* vibe and never bothered to approach. By opening herself up to Declan, was she suddenly sending out vibes that told people she wasn't as untouchable as she had previously worked hard to appear?

"HE'S STILL HERE." Declan sat across from Gage in the sergeant's office, a space as familiar as his own cubicle back in Denver with its stacks of files, bulletins pinned to the wall and framed commendations mixed with family photos on the credenza. Gage had explained that the sheriff was away for two weeks and Gage was in charge of the case.

"Barclay's here. In Eagle Mountain." Gage didn't try to hide his skepticism.

"Or close," Declan said. "He's found a place to stay and he probably has a job. Bartender. Waiter. Janitor. Store clerk. Some position that businesses always need to fill. He'll be a model employee. Everyone will like him. If you ask them to describe him, they'll say ordinary or average. Sometimes women say he's good-looking. They'll talk about his nice smile or his nice eyes. But his eyes won't be their real color. He'll wear contact lenses. He'll have cut his hair, maybe dyed it. Or he'll wear a wig. He'll grow sideburns or a goatee. Once, he plucked his eyebrows and used makeup to sharpen his jawline and cheekbones. I don't know where he learned to do that—he doesn't show any history of having acted or been involved behind the scenes in theater, but he's good."

"Why do you think he's in Eagle Mountain?" Gage asked. "Or nearby?"

Declan clenched and unclenched his fists, trying to control his frustration. Gage didn't know the whole story. And he didn't know Declan. He had a right to be skeptical. "Because it's what he does—what he's done every time he's killed on the spur of the moment," he said. "He stays in the area, finds a target and plans his next murder. I don't know if it's a compulsion or a game he likes to play with the cops, but it's what he's done at least twice. I think it's three times, but he was never connected to a first victim who started the pattern."

"Eagle Mountain is a small town," Gage said. "New people stand out."

"But you have new people all the time. It's a popular area. A tourist spot. You must have people drift in and out."

Gage nodded. "You're right. But we try to notice, especially if we think they might be trouble."

"Barclay won't be like that. He never makes trouble, and he's not one to stand out."

"He just kills people." Gage's voice was flat.

"He kills women," Declan said. "And it will be just one. Then he'll move on. That's what he's always done before."

"One is one too many."

"It is. I want to stop him."

The sergeant didn't answer right away. Instead, he fixed Declan with a steady, brown-eyed gaze, as if daring him to defend himself. Declan waited. "You're officially on leave," Gage finally said. "Your boss made a point of telling me that."

"Yes, and before that, I was on vacation." So that was established—he and Gage both knew he had no business looking for Terrence Barclay.

"Why isn't the town swarming with federal marshals, here because Barclay is here?" Gage asked.

He had wondered how long before they got to that question. "Because they don't believe in the pattern." He sat back and sighed. "I told you I never found a first, spontaneous victim before Barbara Racine, the first woman he was convicted of killing, in Helper, Utah. Prosecutors were able to show that he stalked her for weeks before he strangled her. His next conviction was for the murder of Selena Ferguson, in Boise, Idaho. He worked in her office for three months before he killed her. Signs pointed to his having planned that murder as well."

"What about the spontaneous killing you say set him off?" Gage asked.

"Darlene Castleburg. She was shot in Boise when someone stole her car. I think it was Barclay, but he didn't leave any evidence behind. Authorities in Idaho arrested a known car thief and charged him with the crime. I think they got the wrong man."

Gage shifted in his chair and leaned forward. "All right. You say there was one other?"

"He murdered Deputy Marshal Glenda Zanett when he escaped my custody," he said. "That happened near Wellington, Colorado. A week later he murdered Elizabeth Porterfield. That was the crime where he left her boyfriend to drown in the middle of a flooded river. Barclay stalked the couple on a camping trip and attacked in the middle of the night. He had been stalking her ever since he'd shot Glenda."

"How could a man who must have had every law enforcement officer in the state after him have remained so near where his last crime took place?" Gage asked.

"I told you. He knows how to hide in plain sight. And no one ever expects him to be brazen enough to stay put."

"You told your superiors all of this?"

"Yes. But they think I'm wrong. They don't want to admit they missed him before. Because Elizabeth was killed at a campground two hundred miles from Wellington, they believe that's where Barclay was hiding. But I went to Wellington. I talked to the people there. They remembered a cleaner at a local motel who sounded like Barclay to me—he had shaved his head and wore tinted glasses. A polite, quiet guy who never gave anyone trouble. But the motel—where he also stayed in a room set aside to house employees—was only one block from Elizabeth's apartment."

"It's circumstantial," Gage said.

"A lot of it is. But that doesn't mean it isn't true. And why take a chance? The feds are looking for Barclay everywhere but here. He probably thinks he's safe."

"How are we going to find him?" Gage asked.

"I'd start by making a list of all the people who have shown up in town in the past week," Declan said. "Anybody who has decided to stay. Check new employees of businesses. You can rule out women, but he's good at portraying different ages."

"I don't have the time or the manpower to do that," Gage said. "We're short one deputy. Soon to be two, when Jamie Douglas goes on maternity leave."

"One thing I have a lot of right now is time."

"Barclay knows you," Gage said.

"He does. But law enforcement presence doesn't seem to scare him off. In Boise, he was a waiter at a restaurant where the local sheriff had coffee every morning."

"But the two of you have a history," Gage said.

A history Declan would dearly love to put an end to. "Maybe that will work in my favor." *This time.*

"If he thought you weren't a threat, maybe because you were a murder suspect yourself, he might let his guard down," Gage said.

There was a question in Gage's voice. Declan answered it. "You mean because the locals were naive enough to fall for his setup of shooting that poor woman with my weapon?"

Gage nodded. "You're not at the top of our list for that crime, but Barclay doesn't have to know it. But that would mean the rest of the public wouldn't know, either. For this to work, everyone would have to believe you were still under suspicion. Would you be willing to accept that?"

"Yes. If it means getting Barclay, I don't care what people here think of me." Except one person. He hated to think of Grace believing he was a murderer.

Would she believe that? He didn't think so,

but he would probably never know for sure. Barclay was searching for his next victim. And he was probably watching Declan. No need to bring Grace to his attention.

Chapter Seven

Temperature at 7 a.m. 12F. Wind <5 mph from northeast. Sunrise: 6:24 a.m. No new snow accumulation.

Short-tailed weasel in woodshed. Still in full winter white, except for the black tip on its tail. It was carrying a dead vole; probably unearthed from the burrow behind the woodshed. Goldfinches showing first signs of gold. Mule deer haven't shed antlers yet. Bobcat with two grown kittens from last year's litter passed through shortly before dawn.

Grace turned the page in one of her grandfather's notebooks—this one from January 1972. She pictured him, sitting in this same chair at this desk by the window, recording his observations in his neat handwriting. Every day included descriptions of the wildlife he had seen, of trees and flowers, the water levels of streams and the daily weather. He painted a picture of a rich, colorful world, but his notebooks almost never mentioned people. Occasionally, he would note that she had spotted a particular bird or animal near the cabin—the only indication that she was staying with him at the time. He never mentioned friends or other family members or later, when he became an employee of the research lab, his coworkers.

Yet Grandfather had never seemed unhappy. He had liked his solitary life. Sometimes she envied that. As much as she enjoyed the beauty and autonomy of her position here, she did get lonely. She wasn't one to need a lot of other people around her. One other person would be enough, she thought.

Loud barking from Bear jarred her from her reverie. She hurried to the front window and was surprised to see a snowmobile headed up the drive. Her heart raced as the man driving parked and climbed off the machine, but when he removed his helmet, she stepped back in surprise to see Sergeant Gage Walker.

By the time Gage reached her door, she had quieted Bear and composed herself enough to answer his knock. "Hello, Sergeant," she said.

"Hello, Grace. I need to ask you a few more questions related to Declan Owen."

She had plenty of questions she wanted to ask

him: How was Declan doing? How much longer did he plan to stay in town? Had they found Terrence Barclay? But she stepped back and held the door open wider. "Of course. Come in."

Gage shed his snowmobile suit and left it on a chair on the porch, then followed Grace inside. She sat at her desk chair, while he settled onto the sofa.

"I know you already gave a statement about what happened last Wednesday, but I'd like to go over everything again." He took out a notebook and pen. "Sometimes people remember new details after the initial shock has worn off."

She clasped her hands in her lap, ignoring how clammy they had become. "All right. What do you want to know?"

"Start with your arrival at Dixon Pass and go from there until we showed up Thursday morning."

Once again, she went over the events of those two days. While she had participated in the search for the person who had left the bloody footprints leading away from the car, she hadn't done more than glance into the car. Hannah and one of the volunteers who was a nurse, Danny Irwin, had examined Agnes's body, along with Jake Gwynn, who had been the first law enforcement officer on the scene. "We only searched for about thirty minutes before the storm got too intense for it to be safe on that steep, narrow trail," she said. "I was anxious to get home before the weather deteriorated further."

"Tell me everything that happened when you got home," Gage prompted.

She told him again about the naked, bleeding man stumbling in front of her, how she helped him inside, tended to his wounds and gave him clothing.

"You weren't afraid of this stranger appearing out of nowhere?" Gage asked.

"No." She had wondered about that herself, considering an encounter with a man she didn't know at the natural foods store could make her nervous. "I think I was so focused on taking care of him that I didn't have time to be afraid," she said. "And he never said or did anything threatening. He was injured and confused."

"What did he say about what happened to him?" Gage asked.

"He didn't remember."

"And you believed him?"

His words made her feel sick. "Yes, I believed him," she said. "Trauma can cause memory loss, particularly head injuries. And I really didn't think anyone would voluntarily wander around in a blizzard with no clothes on. Obviously, someone had injured him and left him to die."

"You don't think he could have hit himself in the head and faked his memory loss?"

"That's ridiculous!" She started to stand, then forced herself to sit, to try to calm down. "I'm not a doctor, but that wasn't a tap on the head," she said. "And I've known people who lost their memories after a head injury, so I don't think Declan was faking his amnesia. It would make things a lot easier for him if he could remember what happened, wouldn't it?"

"I guess that depends on what happened," Gage said. "If he killed Agnes Cockrell, saying he doesn't remember and trying to put the blame on someone else would be convenient."

"You can't think he killed her." She rose to her feet, unable to contain her emotions any longer. "He didn't even know her. And he told you who probably killed her—Terrence Barclay. Declan was following him."

"We only have Marshal Owen's word that that's what he was doing," Gage said. "His supervisor says he was on vacation. No one else has seen Barclay."

"He had no reason to kill Agnes," she said. "And no reason to injure himself or to hike two miles from his car, in the mountains, in a blizzard, and show up at my cabin—which he couldn't have even known existed. If I had decided to wait out the storm in town, he would have died before anyone found him."

Gage nodded and closed the notebook. "Thank you for talking to me. I'll let you get back to work now." He rose and she followed him to the door.

"You can't seriously think Declan had anything to do with Agnes's murder," she said. "You should be looking for Barclay."

"I promise you, we intend to conduct a thorough investigation of this crime," Gage said. "In the meantime, we've asked Marshal Owen to remain in town, in case we have more questions for him." He nodded goodbye, stepped outside and a few moments later, he was roaring away.

Grace paced the living room, stomach churning. Declan hadn't killed anyone. How could Gage believe he had? There was a real killer out there, and he might get away with the crime. Worse, he might come back and try to harm Declan. Did Declan have any idea how much trouble he was in?

She went into the mudroom and retrieved her snowmobile suit, then collected her wallet and keys. "I won't be gone long," she told Bear, then headed out to retrieve her snowmobile. Declan needed to know what was going on. And he needed to know he had at least one friend in town who was on his side.

D<small>ECLAN STARTED HIS</small> search for Terrence Barclay at the Alpiner Inn. "Have you had anyone come in looking for work in the past week?" he asked Brit when he found her alone at the front desk on Monday afternoon.

"One of the high school girls, Sarah Jane Utley, asked if we were hiring anyone to work the front desk after school and on weekends," she said. "I had to tell her my husband and I and Hannah take care of that."

"No men looking for work?" Declan asked.

"No. Are you looking for a job while you're here, Marshal?" Her eyes twinkled in a way that had probably charmed many a man in her day.

"No, um, I'm just curious about the employment picture in Eagle Mountain. Do you have a lot of seasonal or transient workers?"

"Oh, some. Especially in summer. A lot of young people come to climb, and they find jobs in restaurants, mostly. Maybe clerking in stores that cater to tourists. Is that what you're talking about?"

"That's it exactly." He leaned on the counter and spoke in a more confiding tone. "If I were looking for someone who might have recently taken a job in one of those places, where do you suggest I look?"

"Are you looking for someone in particular?" she asked.

"Yes, but I can't tell you details."

Her eyes widened. "Oh, I understand. Police business."

He nodded. "But I'm looking for a man, if that helps."

"You could try Mo's Pub or Kate's Kitchen. I think they pretty much always need waitstaff or kitchen help. The Nugget Hotel probably hires a lot of people, too."

"Thanks. I'll see what I can find out."

"I'm happy to help." She smiled, then looked past him and the smile widened. "Hello, Grace," she said. "It's good to see you."

Grace stopped halfway across the lobby. She stared at Declan, then looked away. "Hello," she said, her voice soft and low. He felt the impact of that single word deep in his chest.

He straightened and moved toward her without thinking. "Grace, it's great to see you." Though he had vowed to stay away from her, seeing her now made him feel twenty pounds lighter.

She met his gaze, and he cringed at the hurt in her eyes. What had he been thinking? The woman had saved his life and he had said goodbye and hadn't looked back. "I'm sorry I haven't been in touch," he said, keeping his voice soft, aware Brit was probably listening to every word. "I've had a lot going on."

Grace nodded. "I know." She glanced past him, toward the front desk. "Is there somewhere we can talk?"

He started to invite her for coffee, then thought better of it. As much as he wanted to talk to her, he didn't want to risk Barclay seeing them together. "There's a sunroom in the back," he said. "We can talk there."

He led her to the glassed-in room off the back of the inn. No one else was there, and they settled at either end of a sofa upholstered in nubby blue-and-gray tweed.

"You look much better," she said, studying the bruising at his temple. "How do you feel?"

"I still don't remember anything about what happened at Dixon Pass," he said. That reality was a constant knot in his stomach.

She nodded. "It can be especially frustrating when other people don't believe you can't remember."

She understood that, didn't she? Was that why she looked so sad—remembering her own trauma? "Are you okay?" he asked. "You look upset."

"Sergeant Walker came to see me a little while ago," she said.

"Gage Walker came to see you?"

"He asked me to tell him again everything that happened the day you came here." She leaned toward him, hands knotted at her sides. "He still thinks you killed Agnes Cockrell— that you shot her, then hit yourself in the head and stumbled off into the snow. He thinks you made up the story about Terrence Barclay to divert attention. Even though I pointed out to him how ridiculous that is."

"That was really foolish." Declan hadn't meant to say the words out loud, but really, what was Gage thinking? Sure, they wanted locals— primarily Barclay—to think he was the focus of the sheriff's investigation into Agnes's murder. But why upset Grace this way?

"I'm not under arrest," he said. "The locals are just trying to cover all their bases. They'll realize soon enough I couldn't have killed Agnes. I didn't even know her. Why would I shoot her?"

"I told him that! And there's something else. Something I thought of on the way over here."

"What's that?"

"Agnes's car! It wasn't there when Search and Rescue responded to the scene. There's no way you could have driven it somewhere else and had time to show up outside my cabin that afternoon. The real killer must have stolen her car. I need to tell Gage that."

"He already knows." Declan took her hands. They were ice-cold, so he wrapped both his hands around them. "The sheriff's department found Agnes's car in Delta a few days ago," he said. "Someone had left it in an alley. Gage knows it couldn't have been me."

She sat back but didn't try to pull free of his grasp. He massaged her hands gently, trying to bring some warmth back into them. "Then why did he act as if he was sure you were the murderer?" she asked.

"Maybe he was hoping to throw you off guard, to see if you revealed anything he didn't know."

She slid one hand free and covered her eyes. "I feel foolish, rushing down here like this," she said.

"It's good to see you."

She lowered her hand and met his gaze once more. "Why haven't I heard from you?"

He released her hand and looked away. "My life is such a mess right now. I didn't think it was fair to involve you."

Her laughter startled him. He looked around and she was smiling. "I'm already pretty involved, don't you think?" she said.

He forced himself not to return the smile. As

much as he welcomed her presence, he wouldn't be doing her any favors letting her get closer. "If Gage is telling you those things about me, he's probably told other people, too," he said. "I'm only going to be in Eagle Mountain a little while, but you live here. You don't need your friends and neighbors believing you're friends with a suspected murderer."

"You're not a murderer, and anyone with any sense will realize that." She put her hand on his thigh, and he felt the heat and weight behind the gesture. "I want to help you."

He needed help, but was she really the person to give it? "How are you going to do that?" he asked.

She sat back, the moment of intimacy broken. "I thought maybe we could snowshoe the route you probably took to get to my cabin from Dixon Pass. It's a fun hike in clear weather, and it's possible we'll find something, or you'll see something, that will trigger your memory."

He hesitated but couldn't make himself say no. "That's a great idea," he said. There didn't seem much chance of Barclay seeing them together in the middle of nowhere, and the prospect of anything that might help him remember what had happened, coupled with the chance to spend the day with someone who didn't view him with suspicion, was too much to pass up.

Chapter Eight

Grace had arranged to pick up Declan from the end of the Forest Service road near her cabin on Tuesday morning. She had been surprised to learn he had rented a car. "Should you be driving so soon after a head injury?" she asked.

"I'm doing great," he said, and she didn't press. She had so many other things she wanted to know: What had the sheriff's department told him? What did the Marshals Service have to say? Did he still think Terrance Barclay was in Eagle Mountain?

But she had spent a lifetime keeping questions to herself. It was far easier to let people reveal themselves in their own time. Not always satisfying, but with less potential for rejection.

She was waiting on her snowmobile when the roar of an engine shook the still air. Moments later, a battered green pickup, lifted on oversized tires, growled toward her. It jerked to a halt, engine protesting, then died in a cloud of acrid smoke from the tailpipe. The door shoved open and Declan jumped to the ground.

"This is your rental car?" she asked.

"It was the only thing available at the local garage." He regarded the hulking vehicle. "You don't think it will help me blend in with the locals?"

"I don't know about blending in, but they'll have plenty of warning to get out of your way." She handed him her extra snowmobile helmet. "Are you ready? I figure we'll ride back up to my cabin and start snowshoeing from there."

"Sounds good." He put on the helmet, then collected a day pack from the truck and slipped it on.

She climbed onto the snowmobile and he straddled the seat behind her, then she started the engine and took off.

The steepness of the trail up to her cabin made it impossible to keep any distance between their bodies on the narrow seat. They ended up pressed together, his hands on her waist, his chest against her back. She let herself lean back against him, aware of the muscles of his thighs clenching and unclenching as he leaned into a curve or tried to steady himself. His gloved hands gripped her waist, and she wished there weren't so many layers of clothing between his fingertips and her bare skin.

She was almost sorry when she pulled up to the cabin. Bear stood on the porch, barking and wagging his tail. "Do you remember me?" Declan asked after he had removed his helmet. He held out a hand to the dog, who sniffed it, then accepted a scratch behind the ears.

"I have some snowshoes for you over here," she said and led the way to the end of the porch. She handed him the shoes and poles.

"Did these belong to your grandfather?" he asked.

"Yes. He left me the cabin and everything in it. He wasn't the kind of person to have a lot of excess possessions, so I kept everything. I enjoy reading his books and eating off the same dishes we shared when I was a child." She flushed, wondering if she had said too much. She wasn't usually so talkative. "Does that seem odd to you?"

"It sounds as if this was always a special place for you." He stepped into the snowshoes and bent to buckle the straps. "Why did you come here in the summers?"

"My parents divorced before my first birthday, and my father died not long after that. It was easier for Mom to send me here when school let out than to try to find childcare." Her mother would have been happy to let her live with Grandfather full time, and Grace would have preferred that, too. But he had pointed out there was no way for her to get an education in such a remote setting, in those days before satellite internet and cell phones.

"Where was home when you weren't here?" he asked.

"Little towns all over Iowa. I was always happiest here," she added.

He didn't ask why a child would be happier away from her mother, though he must have wondered. People who had happy childhoods couldn't imagine how unhappy some children could be.

"How are those snowshoes for you?" she asked, anxious to steer the conversation in a safer direction.

He took a few experimental steps. "They should work fine." He looked around them. "Where exactly did you find me?"

"About halfway back down the snowmobile trail to the road." She indicated the direction with her pole. "There's a hiking trail that parallels my property line until it intersects with the road. I think that's probably the path you were following. When you heard my snowmobile, your instincts sent you moving toward the sound—and help."

"I feel like I haven't thanked you enough for

what you did for me that day," he said. "It still hasn't sunk in, how close I came to dying."

"You're obviously a survivor," she said. "I don't know how many people would have made it as far as you did." He had a strong body, of course, but in her short time with Search and Rescue, she had already learned that in dire situations, a strong mind could count for more than physical conditioning.

"I'm curious to see the route you think I took," he said.

"We can start here and intersect the trail." She started out, pausing every ten yards or so to get her bearings. Sun streamed through the bare white branches of aspen trees, making the crystals in the snow sparkle like glitter. Their snowshoes sank half a foot in the fluffy powder before providing steady footing. After a few minutes, she found a rhythm, alternating planting poles and snowshoes, until she was moving with an easy, rocking gait.

"How do you know where you're going in all this snow?" he asked.

"Right now I'm following animal trails and headed in the general direction we need to go," she said. "When we get to the actual trail, it will be easier—you'll see."

"If you say so."

They continued in silence for another ten

minutes, Bear romping alongside with regular side trips into the trees, where he would paw at a fallen log or plunge his whole head into the drifts, emerging with a crown of white fluff and whiskers full of snow.

She stopped and pointed with her pole to a blue metal diamond fastened to the trunk of an aspen to their right. "That's a marker for the trail," she said. "We can follow this all the way to the pass."

Declan frowned at the five-inch-tall marker. "I don't think I would have known to even look for a marker like that," he said. "Much less follow it for miles in a snowstorm."

"You probably didn't." She turned left and resumed their journey up the trail. "But look at how, even with the snow obscuring the trail itself, there's this cleared area between the trees. It's the easiest route to take. Animals know that." She stopped to indicate the imprint of deer hooves in the snow. "Your body would have taken the easiest route."

He studied the landscape around them, while she watched him. The distress on his face clearly telegraphed what he was thinking. "It's okay if nothing looks familiar," she said.

He nodded, put his head down and moved past her.

She let him take the lead, trusting him not

to get lost with the markers to guide him. "You know where I'm from," she said. "Where did you grow up?"

"All over." He glanced back at her. "My dad was an Army general. We moved every few years—Texas, Virginia, Hawaii, Georgia, Germany. I lost count after a while."

"Where are your parents now?" she asked.

"They retired to Arizona."

"They must be so proud of you."

"Mmmm." He stopped and studied the snow at his feet. "I keep expecting to see something to show I was here," he said. "Blood or clothing or something."

"The snow would have covered any blood," she said. "And if whoever hit you took your clothing, you wouldn't be likely to find it out here."

"You're right, but I was hoping for something." He stepped to the side of the trail. "You'd better lead the way again."

They were the first ones—besides local wildlife—to use the trail since the snowstorm, and she tried to focus on the beauty of the silent landscape and the pristine snow. A gray squirrel fussed from a branch overhead, setting Bear to barking, dancing on his hind legs in a futile attempt to reach the furry little varmint. Farther up the trail, a snowshoe hare startled from beneath a currant bush, big feet flashing behind him as he bounded away. After about an hour, they left the cover of the trees. The trail seemed to stop altogether at the edge of a cliff.

Grace stopped and looked down on the rushing waters of Grizzly Creek ten feet below, a noisy cascade pouring between blocks of ice.

"What now?" Declan asked, joining her at the cliff edge.

"The trail heads up this way." She indicated a ledge alongside the water that climbed steeply upward.

"I came down that? In a snowstorm?" he asked.

"It's pretty amazing, but it's the only way down here," she said.

He shook his head but followed her toward the ledge. "You can't see them now, but in the summer there are steps here," she said, and sidestepped up the steep slope.

"How did I not fall into the creek and drown?" he asked.

"Like I said—you're a survivor. You have good instincts."

"Or maybe it was just a case of ignorance being bliss. I had no idea of the danger, so I just kept going."

"I guess that's a survival instinct, too," she said.

They didn't talk much after that, as the trail

became even steeper and they needed all their breath to make it up the slope. Before much longer, they could see the road above them and hear the occasional passing car.

They emerged onto the roadway less than twenty yards from where his car had been parked. Declan kicked off his snowshoes and walked to the pullout, the ruts made by the wrecker that had towed his car still visible.

Grace turned to look out across the valley, leaving him to his thoughts. She had a spectacular view of snowcapped peaks rising above the sparkling creek, against a sky as blue and clear as a sapphire.

Declan moved up alongside her. "You would think I would remember a view like this," he said.

"I don't think anyone knows how the brain really works," she said.

He turned his back on the view, and she turned with him. "I can imagine how it all happened," he said. "The woman, Agnes Cockrell, must have stopped here for some reason. Maybe to look at the view, or maybe something was wrong with her car. Barclay saw her and stopped. Maybe he offered to help her or was just a friendly guy, also admiring the view. But then he grabbed her. He would have waited until I was approaching, so that I would see and stop to help. I'm not sure how he overpowered me and got my gun, but he did. He shot Agnes and hit me in the head—probably with the gun. While I was out, he stripped me and pushed me over the edge. I landed on the trail. He put Agnes's body in my car. He drove his car back down the road to Carson Canyon, then walked back up and took her car and drove it until he ditched it in Delta."

"He took a really big chance of being seen," she said.

"Not so much. He had stolen the car he was driving, so it wasn't linked to his name. If someone saw Agnes's car parked near mine and stopped to investigate, they would have found her body. They might or might not have found me. Barclay could have seen what was happening and headed another direction. Eventually, someone would have picked him up. No one would know he had just assaulted a US marshal and killed a woman."

"Have you told the sheriff's department all this?" she asked.

"Yes, but it doesn't matter what I think happened if I can't remember what actually happened." He gripped his head with both hands and groaned. "Why can't I remember?"

She hated seeing him so distraught. "I know it's hard," she said. "But please don't beat yourself up over this. It really isn't your fault." Even as she said the words, she knew how difficult they were to believe.

"How do you live with the not knowing?" he asked. "How do you accept there's this blank in your life you can never fill in?"

"I don't know that you ever accept it," she said. "You just…learn to live with it. Maybe it helps that it happened to me when I was so young." Though sometimes she wondered if that hadn't made the experience even worse.

"What happened? Can you tell me?"

She could say no. It wasn't something she talked about. But she felt his pain—and the fear behind it. If anyone understood what she had experienced, it would be him.

"I was nine years old," she said. "My mother was driving me to a swimming lesson. My little sister was in a car seat beside me in the back. Hope was three. The car left the road and hit a utility pole. Hope was killed and I was seriously injured. I was in a coma for five days, and even after I woke up, I didn't really remember anything for weeks after." She looked into his eyes, letting him see the bewilderment that still lingered after all this time. "All I know from two months before the accident until three months after is what my mother and the doctors and therapists told me. My therapists said my brain was protecting me from the trauma, but how could what really happened be worse than my doubts and imaginings?"

He opened his arms and she moved into his embrace, her head resting against his shoulder. He held her so tightly, so securely. She closed her eyes and surrendered to this feeling of being so protected. So treasured.

A blaring horn from a passing truck on the highway made them jerk apart. "We'd better head back," she said and turned to collect her poles from where she had rested them against a mile marker.

The trip back went more quickly, the downhill grade and packed trail giving them momentum. Bear walked between them, tongue hanging out, too tired now to follow the scents of wildlife.

They emerged on the snowmobile trail and made their way back up to her cabin, where they kicked off their snowshoes.

She was about to invite him in for coffee, but he spoke first. "Thank you for telling me your story," he said.

"I don't talk about it much," she said. "But I knew you would understand."

He put his arms around her, and it seemed the most natural thing in the world to move closer. And even more right to tilt her head up for his kiss. He kissed like he knew this was what she had been waiting for—and what he had been waiting for, too. His mouth teased awake nerve endings she hadn't known existed, and she leaned into him, greedy to feel more, take more, be more. She gripped his arms, to hold herself up and to keep him near. She was greedy and didn't care if he knew it. But then, he was greedy, too, angling his mouth more firmly against her and shaping his hands to the curve of her hips to bring her even closer.

She was smiling when he broke the kiss, but the burning look he sent her could have melted her right there in the snow. "I'd better go," he said.

"I can take you." She turned toward the snow-mobile.

"That's okay. I think the walk would do me good." He touched her chin and studied her lips as if he might kiss her again. Then he turned abruptly and stalked away.

She hugged herself and watched him go, her blood still fizzing like champagne.

Chapter Nine

On Wednesday, Declan began his search for Terrence Barclay at the Nugget Hotel, clearly the largest lodging establishment in town. About half the building appeared to be under construction, with workmen moving in and out, the sounds of power tools filling the air. He stopped to study the scene. Almost any of the workers within his sight might have been Barclay—young, white, of average height and build. He studied the face of each man who passed. He had spent enough time with Barclay that he thought he could recognize him, but none of the men here looked familiar. Others before him had thought they could recognize Barclay, too, and the murderer had managed to slip past them.

"Can I help you with something?" A thin-faced man in a blue suit addressed Declan. A pin on his lapel identified him as *R. Guidry, Manager.*

"I'm a US marshal, tracking a fugitive," Declan said. "Maybe you can help me." At this point, he would normally pull out his credentials, but since that wasn't an option, he was going to have to bluff his way through this.

"Do you have some identification?" Guidry asked.

"I'm working undercover," Declan said. "But you can telephone the Rayford County Sheriff's Department and they'll confirm I'm with the Marshals Service." At least, he hoped they would.

Guidry studied him for a long moment, then pulled out a cell phone. He scrolled through it, hit a button to dial and waited while the call went through. Declan pretended to study a brochure on the county and tried not to fidget. Guidry identified himself, then said, "I've got a guy here, says his name is Declan Owen. He says you can confirm he's with the US Marshals office." Pause. "Uh-huh." Another pause. "Yeah, that's him. Okay. Thanks." He ended the call and looked back up at Declan. "Let's go into my office, Marshal."

He followed the manager into a small office to the left of the front desk and took a seat in the only chair other than the one behind the desk where Guidry settled. "Who is a US marshal looking for in Eagle Mountain?" Guidry asked.

"His name is Terrence Barclay," Declan said. "But he won't be using that name. Caucasian, fair-skinned, twenty-seven, five feet nine inches tall, about one hundred fifty pounds. He's been known to change his hair and eye color. Do you have any new employees, hired within the last week, who fit that general description?"

"What's this man done?" Guidry asked.

"He's murdered three women and is suspected in the murders of several others."

Guidry's mouth tightened. "We don't have any new employees who fit that description," he said. "Though as descriptions go, it's pretty vague."

"What about the construction crews? Anyone new there?"

"You would have to check with them. Why are you asking these questions instead of the sheriff's department?"

"Barclay escaped from federal custody," Declan said.

"I don't think I can help you. Sorry."

"Do you mind if I talk to some of the staff? Maybe they know someone I should take a closer look at."

"You're free to talk to anyone you want on their own time, but I don't need you to disrupt their workday."

Declan wanted to point out that as a federal officer he was entitled to disrupt anyone's workday but decided not to push it. Technically, he was on leave and wasn't working any case, much less the one involving Barclay. But it annoyed him that this man seemed to put the operation of his business ahead of tracking down a killer.

He stood. "I'm sorry to have disturbed you."

He left the hotel and headed back out into the kind of brisk day that winter vacationers dreamed of—blue skies, pristine snow glistening like sugar, distant mountains making every photograph look like a postcard. But all Declan could think of was how difficult it was going to be to find Barclay before he killed again. Especially if everyone he talked to gave him a reception like R. Guidry.

He spotted the sign for Mo's Pub and went inside. He sat at the bar and an older woman with curly blonde hair approached. "What can I get you?"

He studied the menu on the chalkboard behind the bar. "I'll have a bowl of the Irish stew. Water to drink."

"Coming right up." While he waited for his food, he studied the waitstaff: a young woman and an African American man. There would be other workers, of course, working other shifts or out-of-sight in the kitchen. He could find the manager and go through the same spiel he had given Guidry, but he was liable to get the same reception. Maybe he was going about this all wrong, playing the cop card. He needed a better story.

The bartender returned and slid a large bowl of stew, several packets of crackers and a glass of water in front of him. "Thanks," Declan said. She started to turn away, but he said, "I wonder if you can help me. I'm trying to help a friend back in Ohio find his brother. Last time they were in touch, the brother said he was headed to Eagle Mountain."

"What's the brother's name?"

"His real name is Joe, but he might be using a different name." He leaned forward and lowered his voice. "He was in a little trouble back home and said he wanted to make a fresh start. My friend just wants to make sure he's okay."

The bartender gave him a skeptical look. "What does your 'friend's' brother look like?" she asked.

He described Terrence Barclay. "He might have taken a job in a restaurant—he's done that before."

She shook her head. "Nobody around here like that. Everybody who works here has been around for a while now. Years, even." She looked up as another man approached. "Hey, Mike," she said. "How are you?"

"I'm doing well, Cherise. How are you?"

"I'm good. You want some lunch?"

"Yeah. Can I get a chicken sandwich and fries to go?"

"Sure thing."

Mike—twentysomething, about five-nine, with dark hair shaved at the back and long on top—came to stand beside Declan. Declan's heart beat faster. This could be Barclay—different hair style, a bit thinner than he remembered. His nose looked different, but that could be faked, too, couldn't it?

"Are you okay?" Mike asked.

"You look like someone I know," Declan said.

Mike grinned. "No kidding? Is your friend from Michigan?"

"He might be."

An odd answer, but Mike didn't blink. "That's where I'm from," he said. "I haven't been in town long, actually."

Declan sipped water, forcing himself to remain calm. "How did you end up in Eagle Mountain?" he asked.

"I thought I was just passing through, but I liked the looks of the place. My dad's college buddy owns the natural foods store, so he gave me a job and a place to stay. Who's this guy I look like?"

Declan met Mike's gaze and held it, but the young man didn't flinch. Could this be Barclay, so guileless and forthcoming?

"Hello, Declan."

Declan broke off his staring contest with Mike and turned to see Gage Walker striding toward him. "I'm glad I found you," Gage said. He slid onto the stool on the other side of Declan as Mike turned away. "I've been looking for you."

"Why is that?" Declan asked.

"I got a call from the manager of the Nugget Hotel. He said you were over there asking questions."

"I asked if he had anyone working for him who met Barclay's description." Declan kept his voice low, though Mike had moved away, to the end of the bar.

"Hey, Gage." The bartender was back. "What can I get for you?"

"Cheeseburger and fries," Gage said. "Medium rare, extra-sharp cheddar." When she was gone, Gage turned to Declan once more. "This isn't going to work if you go around upsetting people."

Declan shook his head and glanced down the bar, where Mike was accepting a bag from the bartender. "What do you know about him?" he asked and nodded to Mike.

Gage leaned around Declan to study Mike. "New clerk at the natural foods store," he said. "And I already checked him out. His dad and Arnie, the guy who owns the store, went to college together."

"You know that for sure?"

"Arnie said so. Why would he lie?"

Declan turned his attention back to the stew. It was cooler but still delicious. Mike left with his lunch. Declan stared after him. Why did he have to be hunting a man who was so ordinary he was practically invisible? He turned back to Gage. "Speaking of upsetting people, why did you question Grace and let her think I was your chief suspect in a murder?" he asked.

"Because you are."

Declan glared at him.

Gage shrugged. "I figured she would tell all her search and rescue friends and that would help establish your reason for staying in town."

"You didn't have to upset her that way."

Gage grinned. "So you two are still seeing each other?"

"She came to the Alpiner to find me after you talked to her. You really shook her up." *And then we spent the day hiking and ended up getting way closer than is good for either of us.*

Gage sobered. "I didn't mean to do that. For what it's worth, she defended you. She's certain you're innocent."

The bartender slid a plate in front of him. "Can I get you anything else?" she asked.

"No, thanks, Cherise. This looks great."

They ate in silence for a few minutes. "What have you found out?" Gage asked after a while. "Any likely candidates for Barclay?"

"No. What about you?"

"No. We did find out a couple of things about Agnes Cockrell."

"Such as?"

Gage dragged a french fry through ketchup. "Her husband has never heard of you."

"What did you tell Agnes's husband about me?" Declan asked.

"I didn't tell him anything about you, just asked if he knew you or if his wife knew you."

"So when he hears some gossip that I'm your chief suspect for her murder, is he going to come after me?"

"He's not that kind of guy."

"Does she have any friends or relatives who are that kind of guy?"

"Are you having second thoughts? Are you thinking of leaving town?"

"I can't leave. Not until we find Barclay."

Gage popped the fry into his mouth and

chewed. He waited until he swallowed, then said, "He told us Agnes fell on skis last week and banged up her shoulder."

"How is that significant?"

"When we got a chance to go over her car, we found a flat tire in the trunk. The spare was on the right passenger side. The jack was muddy."

"Like it had been used to jack up a car on a snowy roadside," Declan said. "She had a flat. She couldn't change it herself because of her injured shoulder. She flagged down Barclay for help, and he killed her."

"That area is a dead spot for cell coverage," Gage said. "But if Barclay did stop, where do you come in?"

"I would have stopped to help if I had seen a woman with a flat tire," Declan said.

"But you said Barclay was ahead of you—you were following him."

"Yes."

"Are you sure? Do you remember?"

"I remember following him." He had a clear memory of driving down a mountain road, his gaze fixed on the vehicle ahead, knowing that Terrence Barclay was the driver.

"Did he know you were following him?"

He hesitated. "Maybe?"

It was Gage's turn to remain silent. Waiting.

"He may have spotted me at the motel in Purgatory," Declan admitted. "I thought I ducked out of his way in time—but he may have seen me."

"But you kept following him?"

"I wasn't going to approach him. I was going to see where he ended up and report his location to the Marshals Service."

"Why didn't you do that in Purgatory, if you knew he was at the motel?"

"As soon as I knew it was him, I called a marshal I'm friends with who was on the case. He said they would have someone check it out, but Barclay left before they could send anyone. I followed him."

"And he may have known you were behind him."

"I didn't think so, but maybe."

Gage ate the last of his burger, then pushed the ketchup-smeared plate away. "Do you think he would use Agnes as a decoy—maybe keep a gun on her and have her flag you down?"

"He would absolutely do something like that."

"Do you remember anything like that?"

He wanted to remember. He could picture how the scene would look, but he knew the difference between imagining and remembering. "I don't know for sure," he said. "I can't say for certain that's what happened."

Gage grimace. "So, bottom line, we don't

know if Barclay really is in town or in the next state."

"If he's following his usual pattern, he's here," Declan said.

"A pattern you are apparently the only person to see."

"So, what are you suggesting?" Declan asked. "We do nothing and wait for another murder?"

"I'm not saying that. But it would be helpful if you could remember what happened up there on the pass."

"Except I can't."

The two glared at each other. Declan seethed, but all his anger wasn't directed at Gage. He was furious with himself, too, for his mind's inability to reveal what they needed to stop Terrence Barclay.

"You don't think you've gotten into enough trouble, going after Barclay after you were removed from his case?" Gage asked.

Was that what this was about? Gage didn't like that Declan disobeyed orders from a superior. Declan didn't like that, either, but what choice did he have? "Let me ask you something. If you believed you knew what a killer was likely to do next, even if no one believed you, wouldn't you do everything you could to try to prevent him from murdering again?"

"I guess my first question would be to ask

myself if my obsession with this killer had skewed my vision. Had I let my desire to regain my reputation or get revenge for the way he had made a fool out of me before cloud my judgment?"

"The best way to regain my reputation would have been to walk away, keep my nose to the grindstone and work hard to get back in the good graces of my superiors at the Marshals Service," Declan said. He could tell himself otherwise, but he knew in his gut this was the truth. "What I'm doing now is pretty much professional suicide."

"Then why do it?"

"Because I don't want another woman to die. Wouldn't that be a good enough reason for you?"

Gage nodded. "Yeah. Yeah, it would."

"Then what are we going to do?" Declan asked.

Gage sighed. "You're free to spend your time as you like," he said. "Keep digging into this, but I don't want any more complaints from locals about your snooping around."

"So digging, but no snooping."

"You can snoop, just be more subtle."

Declan didn't bother pointing out that he didn't do subtle very well. He preferred a straightforward approach to protecting the public, but being shuffled aside on this case had eliminated his ability to do that. "I'll be careful," he said. "But I won't stop looking."

"Neither will we." The hard edge to Gage's voice lifted Declan's spirits. Maybe he wasn't in this alone. But would the two of them be enough to defeat Barclay?

Chapter Ten

The message from Search and Rescue had asked anyone available to report to SAR headquarters at 10:00 a.m. Thursday for a "nonemergency rescue call."

"You know what that means, don't you?" Hannah asked as she and Grace stood together on one side of the concrete-floored central room of the headquarters building.

Grace shook her head. "No. How can a rescue call be a nonemergency?"

Hannah leaned in closer. "It usually means a body retrieval." At Grace's stricken look, she nodded. "I know. Not anyone's favorite call. But it's still important to the person's family. Try to remember that."

"Yesterday morning, the sheriff's department got a call from some skiers near back-country hut number three about a body in the canyon visible from the top of the ridge," Sheri said as she stood at the front of the room and indicated a spot on the map of the county behind her. "They said the person was half-buried in snow and not moving. Sheriff's deputies checked things out with binoculars and reported that, from the condition of the body, it's been there awhile."

"What do you mean, 'condition of the body'?" someone on the other side of the room asked.

Sheri frowned. "The deputy told me the skin was white and frozen-looking and a couple of fingers that were visible were broken off."

Groans went up around the room. "Who is it?" Eldon Ramsey asked.

"We don't know," Sheri said. "The sheriff doesn't have any record of anyone reported missing. Hopefully, whoever it is will have some identification. Our job is to get down there and bring the body out." She paused and surveyed the room. "It's a technical climbing area. If you aren't certified for that work, you can opt out, but we need support people up top, and while these aren't pleasant calls, we are called upon to do them from time to time. It wouldn't hurt to get one under your belt."

Grace nodded. The idea of handling dead bodies wasn't pleasant, but she could see how retrieving someone from an isolated grave in the middle of nowhere could bring comfort to family members. "I'll go and do what I can," she said. The other rookies all agreed.

"Great," Sheri said. She turned back to the map. "We can park here." She indicated an area set aside for backcountry skier parking. "From there we'll hike to this saddle, then down-climb from there into the valley. We'll have to carry the body up on a litter. Ryan, I want you with me on the descent. Eldon and Tony, you handle the ropes up top. Danny, you're incident commander. Now, let's head out. The sheriff's department will meet us there."

Grace helped haul ropes and other equipment to the modified Jeep, known as the Beast, used for rescue work. This second incarnation of a rescue vehicle featured a heavy-duty engine, large treaded tires and extra low gears to allow it to climb steep terrain. It also had a winch, a telescoping boom and other equipment to make it useful for rescue work.

While Sheri and several others loaded into the Beast, Grace, Hannah and two other rookies—Nancy and Todd—followed in Grace's Jeep. Navigating the often unmaintained Forest Service road up toward her cabin had given her plenty of experience driving in the mountains, and she had no difficulty piloting them to the remote location from which they would start their mission.

A sheriff's department SUV awaited them at the parking area. Sergeant Gage Walker and a deputy got out of the vehicle and walked toward them. Grace felt a little nervous around Gage after their last encounter, but he nodded at her affably before turning to Sheri. "You can see the body two-thirds of the way down the slope, in deep snow," he said and handed her a pair of binoculars.

Grace followed the others to the edge of the dirt road, where the landscape fell away into a steep valley. She squinted and thought she could make out a patch of bright red, like a hat or scarf, though it was too far below to make out clearly. "How are they ever going to get down there?" she asked Nancy.

"They will," Hannah said from behind them. "But I'm just as glad it's not me making the climb."

Sheri looked up at the sky. "We don't have too many hours of good light in this valley," she said. "We'd better get started."

Grace joined the others in unloading gear, then watched as Ryan demonstrated how to set anchors for the climbing ropes and reviewed the procedure for rigging lines. Even in the middle of an operation, the veterans took the time to teach the rookies.

"Hello, Grace."

Sergeant Walker had approached her from behind. "Hello, Sergeant," she said.

"Declan tells me I upset you the other day," Gage said. "I didn't mean to do that."

The apology left her speechless. "I'm fine," she managed.

"We have to gather as much evidence as we can whenever there's been a crime," Gage said. "Especially one of this magnitude. That means asking hard questions."

She nodded. "I understand."

"Declan has worked in law enforcement long enough to understand how things are," Gage said. "You don't need to worry about him."

Worry wasn't the first word she thought of when it came to her feelings for Declan Owen. Concern, maybe. Attraction, certainly. Along with a little fear—not of the man himself, but of how vulnerable she felt when she was with him.

"We've asked Declan to remain in town while we complete our investigation," Gage said.

"How long will that be?" How much longer would she get to see him?

"It could be several weeks. Has he told you he's on leave with the Marshals Service until then?"

She shook her head. They hadn't discussed his work outside of his search for Terrence Barclay.

"Grace, come give me a hand with this!" Sheri called.

"I have to go," she said and hurried away from Gage. She couldn't imagine why he had told her those things about Declan. Was it because Declan had asked him to?

For the next several hours, she and the other volunteers were absorbed in the retrieval of the body in the valley far below. Though the sun had been high overhead when they began the operation, the surrounding mountains soon cast long shadows and the temperature dropped until Grace was shivering in spite of her layers of winter clothing. She stood with half a dozen other volunteers and watched Sheri and Ryan make the long, slow descent. The snow came to their knees in places, and they had to maneuver carefully around hidden rocks. Once the two climbers were in place, a litter would be sent down to them, then they would reverse the process, bringing the litter up behind them.

Grace tried not to think about what they would have to deal with when they reached the body. Loading a frozen corpse into the litter didn't sound like a pleasant, or an easy, task. She said as much to Hannah.

"At least they don't have to worry about hurting the poor person any more on the way up," Hannah said.

After two hours, Sheri was within a few feet of the body, Ryan not far behind. The radio Danny was using to communicate with the two of them crackled and popped. "You are not going to believe this!" Sheri said.

Ryan's comment was more succinct—a single swear word, loud and clear over the radio.

"What's going on?" Danny asked.

"We didn't go to all this trouble for a body," Sheri said. "It's a mannequin."

"Repeat that," Danny said. "I don't think I heard correctly."

"Somebody put a mannequin down here," Sheri said. "All dressed up in winter gear."

"Somebody's idea of a sick joke," Danny said.

"It gets sicker," Ryan said. "I took a look and this dummy is seriously messed up. Like—mutilated."

Danny looked around and motioned Gage to come over. "You need to hear this," he said and handed the radio to Gage.

"This is Sergeant Walker," Gage said. "What have you found down there?"

Ryan explained about the mannequin, then Sheri cut in. "Someone did this on purpose. They cost us a lot of time and expense, not to mention endangering volunteer lives."

"If we can find out who did this, we'll be

sure to charge them," Gage said. "What are you going to do about the mannequin?"

"We're going to bring it back up with us," Sheri said. "We can't leave it down here, littering up the place."

"Besides, if we leave it, we're bound to get more calls," Ryan said. "From a distance, it really did look like a person."

"When you get it up here, I want to take a closer look," Gage said.

It took over an hour to make the climb back up with the mannequin on the litter in tow. When Sheri and Ryan hauled the litter over the edge, the others gathered around to look. Someone had carefully dressed the female dummy, complete with long blonde hair, in snow pants and parka and a bright red knit cap. But then they had carved deep slashes into the torso and across the face.

"That's horrible!" Hannah cried and turned away.

"We'll take this into headquarters," Gage said. "Maybe we'll find some evidence linking this to whoever did it."

"When you do, I'd like to give them a piece of my mind," Sheri said.

"I'd like to do more than that," Ryan muttered.

Gage and his deputy took charge of the mannequin while the volunteers gathered their gear and loaded it back into the vehicles.

Grace and Nancy were walking back to her Jeep when a man skied toward them. "What's going on?" he asked. "Is someone hurt?"

Grace recognized the young man in the orange cap she had met at the gas station. "No one is hurt," she said.

"So, what are you all doing up here?" he asked.

"It's just a training exercise," Nancy said. "Who are you?"

"I'm Tommy," he said. "I came up to see. It's a gorgeous day, isn't it?" He grinned at Grace. "You're the girl from the gas station the other day, right? The one who told me to ask at the library about a place to stay?"

She nodded. "Did you find a place?"

"I sure did. Thanks again for your help."

Awkward silence while Tommy continued to grin at her and she looked everywhere but at him. "I'd better go," she said finally. "Enjoy your day." She turned and headed toward the Jeep.

Nancy caught up. "He was cute," she said. "And he seemed really into you."

"I met him at the gas station—once," Grace said.

"You made an impression on him."

"Yeah, well, he's just visiting for a little while." She wasn't interested in someone just passing through.

Liar. Her conscience pinched her as she thought of Declan. He was in town for a few more days or weeks while the sheriff's department completed their investigation—whatever that meant. But he wasn't going to stick around. Why would he want to, anyway?

DECLAN STARED DOWN at the disfigured mannequin with the sense of having been in this position before. The female figure on the table before him clearly wasn't a real person and there was no blood or bruising, but somehow that made the scene even more macabre. "You say Search and Rescue found this?" Had Grace been there to see the grisly discovery?

"Some skiers saw it, thought it was a body and called it in. It looked real from that far away."

Declan nodded. It looked real enough, even from here. "It's Barbara Racine," he said.

"Barclay's first victim," Gage said.

"The first victim we know about. She's the only one he cut up this way, which led some to believe he wasn't the one who killed her."

"So you think Barclay did this and put the mannequin in that ravine? Why?"

"I don't know. A rehearsal of sorts? Because he wants to wind us up? Or he needed a release of tension. A profiler might be able to tell you."

"No profilers here," Gage said. "He was taking a chance someone would even spot her."

"I heard it's a pretty popular backcountry ski area," Declan said. He had talked to locals enough to know that. "Remote enough that he could get the mannequin there and toss it over without being seen but count on someone discovering it eventually. And if they didn't, it wouldn't make that much difference to him."

"You don't think so?"

"I don't. I think he's just amusing himself right now, until he strikes for real."

"I spoke to your office about this," Gage said.

Declan tore his gaze away from the mannequin. "What did they say?"

"They said they doubted this had anything to do with Terrence Barclay. They suggested it sounded like high school students."

"I suppose they told you not to listen to me," Declan said.

"Something like that." Gage regarded the mannequin. "It does sound like something high school students might do, though if I knew who, I would seriously suggest counseling. The mannequin—sure, they might think throwing it into that valley was funny. But the slashing?" He shook his head. "Maybe, but…"

"But this looks like Terrence Barclay to me," Declan said. "I know you've only got my word against the rest of the Marshals Service."

Gage turned with his back to the table. "I can't see any reason for you to lie to me," he said. "Which doesn't mean I think you're right, but I'm not ready to dismiss everything you say outright."

"I appreciate that."

"You're not winning any friends back at the Marshals Service."

"We've already established that."

A tap on the door interrupted them. "Yes?" Gage called.

Adelaide opened the door. "There's a woman to see you, Sergeant," she said. She glanced at the mannequin and looked away. "It's about Agnes Cockrell."

"I'll see her in my office," Gage said. He offered a hand to Declan. "I'll be in touch."

Declan took Gage's hand with a firm grip of his own, then left. He was halfway across the street when Adelaide hurried after him. "The sergeant wants you to come back," she said.

He followed the office manager back into the sheriff's department and down the hall to

Gage's office, where a plump, pretty blonde sat with a pink-cheeked baby on her lap.

"I thought you might want to hear what Mrs. Waring has to say," Gage said.

Declan nodded. He noticed Gage hadn't bothered to introduce him, which was probably just as well, in case Mrs. Waring had heard any rumors about his involvement in Agnes's death.

"Go ahead, ma'am," Gage said. "Repeat what you told me."

"I saw a notice online that the sheriff's department was looking for anyone who saw Agnes up on Dixon Pass the day she died." She jostled the baby in her arms. "I did."

"You saw Agnes Cockrell on Dixon Pass the day she was killed?" Declan clarified.

Mrs. Waring nodded. "I was driving back from a doctor's appointment, and I passed her. She was on the side of the road with a flat tire. I was looking for a place to turn around and go back to Agnes when Jess here started screaming at the top of her lungs. She was still screaming when I got turned around and drove back, but I saw that a man had stopped. He was standing with her and they were looking at the tire, so I figured I didn't need to get involved. It wasn't as if I was going to be that much help with a screaming baby."

This woman had seen Terrence Barclay, Declan thought. It was possible someone else had stopped to change Agnes's flat tire, but he knew in his gut it was Barclay. "What did this man look like?" he asked. "Would you recognize him again?"

Mrs. Waring shook her head. "I just got a glimpse of his back. I was distracted by the baby. He was wearing a dark coat and a cap and jeans, I think."

This fit the clothing Barclay had been wearing the last time Declan had seen him.

"What was he driving?" Gage asked.

"I'm sorry, I didn't notice." She shrugged. "I don't really notice things like that, and I didn't think it would be important. I was going to call Agnes later and find out how she was doing, but then I heard she had been killed." She bit her lower lip. "Do you think the man I saw killed her? Maybe if I had stopped—"

"It's all right," Gage said. "You didn't do anything wrong, and I appreciate you stopping by. You're helping us to get a better picture of what happened that day."

"I should have stopped," she said. "But I was worried about the baby, and I thought Agnes would be okay." She was working herself up to real tears, Declan thought.

Gage picked up his phone. "Addie, could you help Mrs. Waring to her car?"

Seconds later, Adelaide swooped in and took the distraught woman by the arm. "Come with me and I'll fix you a cup of tea," she said, one arm around the woman's shoulders.

When they were alone again, Gage looked at Declan. "You may think you don't remember what happened," he said. "But I don't think your mind made up that scenario about Barclay using Agnes as a decoy to lure you in. Some part of you knows what happened, even if you can't access it."

"Maybe," Declan said. At least Gage was beginning to believe him.

"Do you think hypnosis would help?" Gage asked.

"I'm willing to try anything."

"I'll do some nosing around, see what I can find out. In the meantime, we're getting a better picture. Now if we could just find Barclay."

Declan returned to the Alpiner Inn, where he changed clothes and sat down to review his case notes again. Maybe there was something in there he had missed.

What he really missed was his office in Denver and access to the databases and support staff he relied on in investigations. Capturing Barclay was going to require more than what he could do alone. He pulled out his phone and called Oscar Penrod.

"Hello, Declan," Penrod said. "Are you back in Denver?"

"No, I'm still in Eagle Mountain," Declan said.

"I assume this means you're still under investigation."

"I didn't murder anyone," he said. "In the meantime, are you sending anyone here to look for Terrence Barclay?"

"Terrence Barclay is none of your concern," Penrod said.

"Is the FBI sending anyone to investigate?" Declan asked. "I'm not part of the search for Barclay, but I do have good reason to believe he's here. Someone who is authorized to do so should investigate."

"You're not part of the search, and how it is conducted is not your concern. That's all I have to say on the matter." *Click!* Followed by silence. Penrod had hung up on him.

Declan threw the phone onto the bed, then began to pace. He'd been right—no one was looking for Barclay in the place where he was most likely to be. No one except Declan, and he had no authority and few resources. Gage had promised to help, but Declan wasn't sure the sergeant even believed his theory that Barclay was in Eagle Mountain and planning to kill again.

What if Declan was wrong? What if the marshals and everyone else was right and Barclay was far away from Eagle Mountain? He stopped pacing. Knowing he had wasted so much time and energy here while Barclay was getting farther and farther away was like a kick in the gut. But he reminded himself that his situation wouldn't be any different if he had realized Barclay was far away. He wouldn't have had the authority to go after him, and after what had happened on Dixon Pass, he would have been foolish to try. He was stuck here in Eagle Mountain until the sheriff's department cleared its murder investigation.

That meant he had nothing to lose by continuing to search for Barclay. If the killer was here, Declan might be the only person standing between him and his next murder.

Chapter Eleven

Declan had every intention of spending the rest of the day combing Eagle Mountain for anyone who might be Terrence Barclay. He couldn't shake the image of that grisly mannequin, fixed up to resemble a real murder victim, and that was enough to motivate his search. But as he drove away from the sheriff's department, he turned away from town, toward the road leading up to Grace's cabin. Had seeing that mannequin shaken her as much as it had shaken him?

The truck he had rented, loud and ugly as it was, negotiated the slush-filled ruts and icy inclines of the Forest Service road with plenty of power, if not a lot of finesse. Declan parked at the end of the road, next to Grace's Jeep. At least he hadn't driven all the way up here only to find her gone. He pulled out his phone, intending to let her know he was here, but of course he had no signal. So he set out walking, following the packed tracks of her snowmobile and the lingering impression of his own boot prints from his visit the day before.

He had left after kissing her because he knew if he didn't walk away, he would end up staying, would end up making promises to her he couldn't keep. He had had plenty of casual relationships in his life and he knew how to handle those, but nothing in his feelings for Grace, confusing as they were, was casual. If he said half of the things that came into his head when he was with her, she would end up thinking he wanted to stay with her forever.

Part of him did want that, but that wasn't possible. His job and general logistics were minor obstacles compared to his fierce inability to make that kind of commitment. He had changed universities twice before he earned his degree, changed jobs four times, moved half a dozen times or more, dated so many women he couldn't remember them all. Every place and every person left him wanting more, though he knew enough to see the biggest lack wasn't in his choice of location and companions, but in himself. All he had to do was give himself a moment of silence and he would hear his father's voice, reminding him how inadequate he was. What woman would want that?

He heard Grace before he saw her. "Come here, boy! Bring me the ball!"

He rounded a curve in the trail and stopped. She stood on the bottom step leading up to her cabin, dressed in a bright red sweater and black leggings, her hair falling loosely around her shoulders. She raised her arm, arced it back, then sent a yellow tennis ball soaring. The dog barked excitedly and bounded after the toy, snow flying up with each leap. He caught the ball and turned to race back toward Grace, who laughed and wrestled it from him to throw again.

She was so beautiful. Strong, capable and clearly smart. Was he the only one who saw her vulnerability? He had seen her wounds and wished he knew who had hurt her.

Bear barked again but this time whirled and bounded toward Declan. He braced himself to meet the dog, but Bear turned again when Grace called him back. "Declan!" She waved and started toward him. "What a nice surprise."

Her smile was enough to rock him back on his heels. "I should have called," he said. "I didn't think about it until I was out of phone range."

"That's okay." She stopped a few feet from him. "Is everything all right?"

"I just wanted to see you." He started toward her cabin and she fell into step beside him, the dog bounding through the snow ahead.

"Is there something in particular you need to see me about?" she asked.

"I heard about the search and rescue call with the mannequin," he said. "Were you part of that?"

Her smile vanished. "Yes. It was creepy. Someone said it must have been a prank, but who would do something like that? Climbing down to retrieve what we all thought was a body was dangerous."

"Did you make that climb?" he asked, trying to hide his alarm.

"No. Sheri and Ryan did it. They're our best climbers. But they could have been seriously injured." They stopped in front of the cabin. "How did you hear about it?"

"Gage told me." At her puzzled look, he added, "We're wondering if Terrence Barclay did it."

Deep lines formed between her brows. "Why would he do something like that?"

"I don't pretend to understand it, but serial killers do strange things." How much should he tell her? He didn't want to alarm her, but he didn't want to leave her in the dark, either. He touched her shoulder and she angled toward him, searching his face. "I told you I think Barkley is here because he intends to kill again," he said.

"Yes."

"His pattern before has been to choose a victim and stalk her. It's always a woman. This thing with the mannequin—it could be a rehearsal or a warning or just a way to relieve tension."

Some of the color left her face, but she nodded. "Are you any closer to finding him?"

"I wish I could tell you yes, but we're not getting anywhere. In the meantime, you need to be careful."

"What? You think he would come after me?" Her voice rose on the last word.

"He picks young, attractive women. Like you. Or like your friends. You should all be careful. You haven't noticed anyone behaving oddly around you, have you? Maybe paying more attention to you than usual?"

She shook her head. "No. Not really." She rubbed her shoulders. "It's getting cold out here. Do you want to come inside?"

"Sure." He couldn't tell if she believed him when he said she might be in danger. Maybe he could persuade her. Or maybe they would find another, more pleasant topic of conversation. Anything to keep her from linking him forever with grisly murders and stalking killers.

Inside, she added wood to the fire, then went into the kitchen and lit the burner on the stove under a teakettle. "Has Gage said anything more to you about Agnes Cockrell's murder?" she asked when she returned to the living room and settled near him on the sofa.

"I think he's beginning to believe that I didn't kill her," he said. "A woman came into the sheriff's department and said she saw Agnes with a flat tire on the side of the road up at Dixon Pass. By the time she turned her car around and went back to help, a man had stopped and was talking to Agnes. The woman had a crying baby with her, so she went on, sure Agnes would be okay."

"Was the man Terrence Barclay, or was it you?" she asked.

The question caught him off guard. He had been so focused on Barclay he hadn't considered that Mrs. Waring might have seen him standing with Agnes. "I'm sure it was Barclay," he said. "Someone drove Agnes's car to Delta, and we know that wasn't me."

"Of course." She hugged her arms across her stomach. "What do you think happened?"

"I think Barclay stopped on the pretext of helping Agnes, then used her as a decoy to get me to stop." He shook his head. "Or maybe I stopped, anyway. I was following Barclay. If I had seen him with anyone, especially a woman, I would have stopped." He put a hand to his head. "If only I could remember." He lowered his hand and studied her. She wasn't exactly serene, but she looked much calmer than he felt. "You really never remembered anything from the accident you were involved in as a child?"

"Nothing." She uncrossed her arms and smoothed her palms down her thighs. "My mother told me over and over what happened on the day of the wreck, but I never remembered. Sometimes I think I do, but I know it's only because I was told the story so often. It's not the same as a real memory."

The teakettle began whistling, and she stood and returned to the kitchen. He watched her go, focused on the lithe body outlined by the clinging knit of her sweater and leggings. He wanted to hold her, not to comfort her so much as to comfort himself, or at least to lose himself for a while in the feel of her body against his.

When she returned moments later with two mugs of tea, he had moved to stand in front of the woodstove and study her desk, stacks of papers neatly arranged on either side of a computer monitor. "How is work going?" he asked.

"It's going well." She handed him a mug, then stood beside him with the other. "Some people might find transcribing all those notebooks boring, but I find it fascinating to read my grandfather's writing."

"You mentioned that he kept weather records. Is there more than that?"

"Much more. He was a true naturalist, interested in everything in the natural world. For more than sixty years he made note every day of what he observed, from weather and temperature to the behavior of local wildlife. It's an extraordinary record that's a remarkable resource for science, from climate researchers to wildlife biologists to meteorologists. It's important work, and I'm so lucky to be a part of it."

"I imagine your grandfather would be proud of you."

"I think he would." She regarded him as she sipped tea. "But the work you do is important, too. Just very different from mine."

"It is important, though I don't know how much longer I'll be doing it."

"What do you mean?"

"My supervisor isn't happy with me. I suppose in his shoes I might feel the same. After Barclay escaped my custody, I was removed from the case. I had no business continuing trying to track him."

"But you found out where he was headed," she said. "Even if you weren't still on the case, that would help the people who were supposed to be looking for him."

"It would have, if they had believed me. But

I'm afraid I've lost all credibility with the marshals office."

"I don't understand."

He blew out a long breath. "I'm an embarrassment. I did something foolish—let a felon get away from me. He got hold of my weapon and used it to kill someone. It's a wonder I wasn't relieved of duty immediately."

"Maybe they didn't want to get rid of a good officer because of a single mistake."

He shook his head. "It wasn't just a mistake. It was a gross failure in my duty."

"How did it happen?" she asked.

He closed his eyes. He had been over the moments so many times in his head, both awake and in his dreams. "He attacked the other marshal I was with, Glenda Zanett. He was shackled, his hands in cuffs, but he turned suddenly and slammed his fists into her face. She went down on her knees. I pulled my gun on him and he headbutted me. I didn't let go of the gun— I'm sure I didn't. But Glenda was still on the floor, screaming, blood running from her face. I turned my head for a fraction of a second to check on her, and Barclay hit me again. I fired, but the shot went into the floor, and then he had the gun."

He fell silent, the scene playing out again in slow motion.

"It's amazing you weren't killed," she said softly.

"He shot Glenda. She had the keys to the shackles, and he stripped them off her belt and managed to undo his own shackles. That's not supposed to be possible, but he must have practiced. I moved toward him, but he shoved the barrel of the gun into my stomach and said he'd kill me if I laid a hand on him. Before I had time to react, he hit me in the head with the gun and I went down. I woke up in a pool of blood, but it wasn't my blood. It was Glenda's."

Grace set aside the tea and put both arms around him. He hadn't realized he was shaking until then. She held him tightly, her head resting on his shoulder, until the tremors subsided. "You couldn't have done anything differently," she said.

"They said I failed in my duty. I failed to safeguard my weapon. I failed to protect a fellow officer." He had heard the words often enough, repeated them often enough that he could say them without emotion. They were just words now, stings that no longer hurt. Or that hurt so deeply he was past acknowledging the pain.

"What did your parents say?" she asked.

He grimaced. "The general said he was ashamed of me."

She gasped and drew back. "Your father said that?"

"It wasn't the first time," he said. "I've been failing to live up to his expectations most of my life."

"What about your mother?"

"She always takes his side."

Her eyes clouded, but not with tears—with anger. "They don't deserve a son like you."

"I think they would probably agree with you."

"I didn't mean—"

"It's all right." He put his fingers to her lips to silence her, and she softened against him once more.

She took his hand and kissed his palm, a feather touch that sent a current of electricity through him. She kissed his wrist above the fabric of his fleece top, then lifted her face and met his lips as he lowered his mouth to hers.

There was nothing timid or withheld in that kiss. She surged to him, pulling him into her with the force of a tide. She gripped the fleece of his top, her nails digging into his shoulders, arching hard against him. He slid both hands around to cup her bottom, then up beneath the soft red sweater, along the curve of her waist to the weight of her breasts in his palms.

She pulled her mouth from his long enough

to stare into his eyes, her pupils dark. "Stay," she said.

"I'm not going anywhere," he said, his voice ragged, and kissed her again.

She tugged off his top somewhere between the woodstove and the door to her bedroom, and by the time they actually reached the bed, they were both naked, their skin hot against the cool sheets. She jerked open the drawer of the bedside table and began rummaging through it.

"What are you looking for?" he asked, only slightly alarmed. He knew a lot of people who kept a weapon in that drawer.

She pulled the drawer out altogether and dumped its contents onto the floor. The sight of her bare bottom up as she clawed through the scattered items sent a fresh jolt of wanting through him, and he moved toward her, but just then she rose up and waved a small packet triumphantly.

"This," she said and thrust the condom at him.

He couldn't help it—he laughed. She glared at him. "I don't see what's so funny about a condom," she said.

"No, but if you could have seen yourself, searching for it…" He chuckled and reached for her, gently this time. "You're beautiful," he said. "Everything about you is beautiful."

She let her gaze slide over him, and a smile erased her look of annoyance. "You're certainly in better shape than the last time I saw you naked." She rested a hand on his hip. "Though even then, I liked what I saw."

"Even blue and shriveled?" he joked.

"Only a little blue. And not shriveled." She slid her hand over to wrap around his erection, and he caught his breath, then gathered her close once more.

They took their time after that, touching and tasting, letting the intensity build again. When she became impatient, he settled her with murmured endearments and touches that teased at what was to come. By the time he unwrapped the condom and rolled it on, his hands were shaking a little, and when she lay back and beckoned him to her, he knew he wouldn't be able to hold back long.

But she knew how to prolong the moment. Maybe all that time sitting quietly, observing nature, had taught her the value of taking her time. She wrapped herself around him and moved with deliberate grace, leading him in a sensual dance. He watched her, mesmerized, as her face transformed and her body tensed. He held her tightly as her climax overtook her, and then he could hold back no more and lost himself to his own satisfaction.

Afterward, they clung together, neither wanting to pull away. "You're pretty wonderful for an abominable snowman," she said.

"So you think maybe I was worth saving?" He slid down to rest his head between her breasts.

"Definitely." She brushed a lock of hair out of his eyes. "Though we could talk about who was saving who."

He wanted to ask what she meant by the words, but it had been a long hike up to her place and more than one sleepless night since he came here. Her bed was warm and she was warmer, and before he could find the right words, his eyes drifted closed and he surrendered to blackness.

Chapter Twelve

Grace woke with the last gray light of dusk filtering through the gap in the bedroom curtains. Declan lay on his back beside her, face slack, jaw dark with beard-shadow, powerful torso pressed against the mattress and outlined beneath the sheet and blanket. He smelled of man and sex, and she wanted to bury her face against his warm skin and breathe in that scent until she was dizzy with it. She was obsessed with him, which felt awkward and silly, but also powerful and amazing.

She eased out of bed and dressed, then went into the kitchen. Bear got up from his bed by the woodstove and followed her, a reproachful look in his brown eyes. "Don't be jealous," she told him and rubbed his ears. "I still love you."

She fed him, then opened the refrigerator and searched for something to make for supper, but her mind refused to consider the practicalities of omelets or soup while Declan lay sleeping in her bed. She marveled at her own boldness, inviting him to stay with her. Everything about him should have threatened her peace of mind—the fact that he was a lawman, if a disgraced one. His amnesia, which only reminded her of the big gap in her own memory. He was too aware and perceptive, the kind of man who was bound to discover all her failings. The kind of person she had always avoided.

Yet she felt safe with him, though *safe* was too passive a term. She felt needed and cherished and giddy with passion.

She was cracking eggs into a bowl when she heard him approaching. She pretended not to notice until he came up behind her and pulled her close. He kissed the back of her neck, sending a shiver through her.

"Are you hungry?" she asked.

"Mmm."

He sent her a wolfish look, and she laughed. "I meant for food."

"That, too." He kissed her again, then drew away, his expression serious. "After we eat, I should head back to town. Not that I wouldn't like to stay, but…"

She nodded. "You have work to do." And maybe they both needed some space to process this hurricane of emotion that had overtaken them. At least, she was pretty sure she did.

"I got a tip about a new waiter at a restaurant between here and Junction," he said. "I want to check him out. You could come with me."

"I don't think so. I have work to do, too." She was supposed to have finished the 1972 notebook by now, but being with Declan had her behind. "Do you want cheese in your omelet?"

"Yes, please."

"The toaster is over there." She nodded across the room. "You can toast some bread while I cook the eggs."

They ate at the little kitchen table, chatting about mundane things. It was nice. Ordinary.

Afterward, she gave him a ride down to his truck. Before he left, she took his arm and gave him a hard look. "Be careful," she said. "This man has attacked you twice. Next time he might kill you." Her voice shook a little at those words.

"I'm not going to let that happen." He kissed her—a deep, thorough kiss she felt all the way to her toes. "I'll call you tomorrow," he said when he finally lifted his head.

"What's going to happen, with us?" She regretted the words as soon as she blurted them out. He would think she was too needy. Moving too fast.

But he didn't look upset. "We'll figure it out," he said.

She waved as he drove away. She wasn't very

adept at figuring things out, but she did know a thing or two about watching and waiting. Her work was all about seeing how things resolved on their own without interference. Whether that was a good approach for relationships, she couldn't say, but it was the only approach she knew.

THE WAITER DECLAN had heard about was not Terrence Barclay. He was too short, with eyes that were too close together to be faked by makeup. Declan spent a discouraging half hour nursing a beer and attempting to make conversation with the bartender about new employees of the restaurant before he gave up and headed back toward Eagle Mountain.

He debated driving up to spend the night with Grace. He wanted to be smart about her, to let his feelings cool a little so he could think sensibly. But she had imprinted herself on his body and all he could think of was getting back into her bed.

A flash of light to his right made him pump the brakes on the truck. He squinted to bring the light source into sharper focus and realized it was the glare off a strip of reflective tape on the back of the parka of a man walking along the side of the road. Declan slowed the truck further and rolled to a stop beside the walker, who was struggling through thick drifts along the side of the county road. "Do you need a ride somewhere?" he asked.

The man, only his eyes visible between a white fleece gaiter and an orange knit hat, took two stumbling steps toward the truck. "That would be great," he said. "I'm supposed to work the overnight shift at the Ranch Motel, and my van wouldn't start."

"Get in," Declan said.

The man climbed into the truck and fastened his seat belt. He hugged himself, then clapped his mittened hands together. Declan realized he was young, but telling anything about his appearance in the darkness was difficult. "What's your name?" he asked.

"Tommy Llewellyn." The man, his hat still hiding his hair and the sides of his face, swiveled toward him. He had lowered the gaiter, revealing a thin mustache above pale, chapped lips.

"Have you been in Eagle Mountain long?" Declan asked, trying to focus on the road, though he kept glancing at his passenger.

"About a week. I've been camping in my van back there." He jerked his thumb in the direction they had come. "I got a job as night clerk at the Ranch, and I'd hate to screw that up my first week."

The hair on the back of Declan's neck rose

up and he tightened his grip on the steering wheel. The timing was right. The easygoing, open manner was typical of the various personas Barclay had assumed. This man had a slight Southern drawl. Oklahoma or Texas? "Where were you before?" he asked.

Tommy sat back again. "I was in Denver for a few weeks before this, but I didn't care for it much. I'm thinking of heading out to Utah soon. I've spent the last year seeing the United States. I live in my van, take a job for a while when I need money. It's a great life."

And a good cover for a fugitive, Declan thought.

"Man, it's cold out there." Tommy settled against the side of the truck cab. "Thanks again for picking me up. I'm about half-frozen." He huddled further into his coat.

He probably was cold if he had been out in the night chill very long, Declan thought. But this was also a good excuse for remaining bundled up. He glanced over at his passenger and thought his eyes were closed. He forced his gaze onto the road again.

He had spent less than two hours with Terrence Barclay previously, and his attention had been directed as much on searching for potential danger from outside as on Barclay himself. As he was described in every bit of court evidence

Declan had read since Barclay had escaped his custody, the man he had been assigned to guard and transport was polite, quiet and cooperative. Inoffensive. Which had probably made him and Glenda let down their guards more than usual and had added to the shock of Barclay's sudden, furious attack upon them.

"Do you like working at the motel?" Declan asked, not because he was interested, but as a way to keep his passenger talking.

Tommy shifted, rousing himself. "It's all right. They have me filing stuff and cleaning the lobby when I don't have customers to wait on, but that doesn't take all night, so I usually watch videos on my phone and stuff like that. It will do until I'm ready to move on."

"Have you met any women since you moved to town?"

Tommy shifted, feet scraping on the floor mat. "It's only been a week. Though there is this one woman I met. Really pretty. Hard to tell what she thinks of me, but if I get a chance, I might ask her out. Why do you ask? Do you have somebody you want me to meet?" No mistaking the teasing note in his voice.

Declan shook his head. "No, I'm just new in town myself. I noticed there are a lot more single men than women."

"That's a lot of places out west, you know?" Tommy said.

A lighted sign up ahead announced the Ranch Motel, and Declan slowed the truck. "You can let me out right up front," Tommy said.

Declan turned into the drive and parked under the portico. "Thanks for the ride," Tommy said, already pushing open the door.

Declan stared at his passenger as Tommy stepped into the harsh glow of the outdoor lighting at the motel entrance. He was pale, acne scarring standing out on his right cheek, bruised half-moons beneath his eyes.

"Is something wrong?" Tommy put a hand to his cheek. "Why are you staring at me?"

Declan looked away. "Sorry. I thought for a minute there you looked like someone I know." Except he didn't. Tommy didn't look familiar to Declan at all.

"I guess we all have a doppelgänger somewhere, right? Thanks for the ride. Maybe I'll see you around."

Then he was hurrying into the motel. Declan put the truck in gear and drove away. He was in no mood to see Grace now. He would spend another evening with the files he had compiled about Terrence Barclay. Was the fact that Declan couldn't remember exactly what he looked like a testament to Barclay's chameleon abilities? Or was it a sign that more than Declan's ability to remember a few hours up on Dixon Pass had been damaged with a blow to his head?

FRIDAY MORNING, Grace walked around the cabin, checking snow depth and moisture content, recording the temperature and observing the progress of bud formation on aspens and the pattern of snow on the mountain peaks visible from her yard. Then she went back inside, poured a second cup of coffee and sat down to fire up her computer and record her observations and submit a report that was due that day.

But the computer informed her there was no internet connectivity. A quick check of her modem showed it to be in working order. Annoyed, she took another slug of coffee, then shrugged back into her coat and boots and went outside to check the small satellite dish attached to the side of her cabin. This was the dish that picked up the signal that provided phone and internet service to her cabin. The dish looked fine, which meant something was wrong with the cell tower or transformer. Though the service was usually reliable, half a dozen times a year she would be without a signal for a few hours or a few days. Last year, the problem had been thieves stealing the batteries that powered the transmitter. Once, an ice storm had broken some equipment. Whatever was going on today would be fixed, and while inconvenient, it wasn't the end of the world. Her grandfather had lived here for six decades with no way to communicate with the outside world, and he had survived just fine.

She returned to the cabin, shed coat and boots, and reheated her coffee and made toast. She ate breakfast while reviewing the final draft of her report, then copied the draft onto a flash drive. She cleaned the kitchen, combed her hair and added a touch of makeup, then donned her snowmobile suit and helmet and slipped the flash drive and her wallet into a pocket. "I'll be back in a couple of hours," she told Bear, who had observed all these actions with the expression of a dog who knew he was going to be left behind. "I'll bring you a treat."

At the library, she signed into one of their computers and sent the report to her supervisor, then answered several emails. She was reading an amusing account of a colleague's encounter with a marmot who stole his lunch when the chair beside her made a loud, scraping noise as it slid back. She glanced over and was startled to see Tommy.

"Hey," he said. "It's good to see you again. How have you been?"

"I've been fine," she answered automatically. Politeness compelled her to add, "How are you?"

"I'm good. I'm working over at the Ranch Motel, and I've got a sweet camp set up down by the river."

She nodded and turned back to the computer, hoping he would get the message that she wanted to be left alone.

"I was wondering if maybe you wanted to go out some time," he said. "We could have dinner or something."

"Oh, um, thank you, but I don't think so."

His smile faltered, then he fixed it back in place. "You're not married or something, are you?" He glanced at her hand. "Except I don't see a ring. But I guess not everyone wears a wedding ring."

"No, I'm not married."

"You've probably got a boyfriend, right? I mean, of course you do."

She thought of Declan. He wasn't her boyfriend. He was a man she had spent one night with. A man she felt a connection to, but that didn't mean she had a claim on him. "I just don't feel like dating anyone," she said. A flash of anger immediately followed these words. Why should she have to explain herself to this man?

"I'm a fun guy, I promise."

She shook her head and focused on the monitor once more. She could feel his eyes on her but didn't dare look his way. She had been in this position before—turning down men who didn't seem able to believe that she didn't want to date them. Friends had accused her of being too picky, but most of them admitted that dating could be uncomfortable and awkward. Grace didn't feel like putting herself through all that.

She waited until Tommy moved away before she shut down her computer and stood. She thanked the librarian on her way out, then, remembering her promise to Bear, she headed to the natural foods store.

Mike was behind the counter. He greeted her with a wide smile. "It's my favorite customer," he said. "How was that chai?"

"It was good," she said.

"Didn't I tell you? What can we get for you today?"

"I just stopped to get some treats for my dog." She headed for the bulk bins in the pet section.

Mike followed her. "What kind of dog do you have?" he asked.

"He's a shepherd mix."

"I love shepherds. Actually, I love all dogs. I wonder if Arnie would let me adopt one."

"Why would he care if you adopt a dog?"

"Well, I'm living upstairs right now. Just until I can find a place of my own."

The door to the storeroom opened and Arnie emerged. A short, round man with a tonsure of brown curls, he reminded Grace of a genial monk. The loose brown sweater he wore only added to this image. "Hello, Grace," he called. "Are you finding everything you need?"

"Yes, I am. Thank you."

Mike moved back behind the counter and began straightening a display of canned olives. Grace bagged up a selection of dog biscuits and walked to the register.

"I was telling Grace here I should get a dog," Mike said to Arnie. "What would you think of that?"

"I think you should be able to support yourself before you add a dog." Arnie moved the bag of dog biscuits onto a scale. "Animals are a big responsibility. You shouldn't adopt one until you're certain you can care for it in the long term."

"You sound just like my dad." Mike laughed. "No wonder the two of you are friends."

"Mike's dad and I met in college and we both worked at an Antarctic research station," Arnie said to Grace. "We were about Mike's age at the time."

"How wonderful that you've kept in touch all these years," she said.

"Dad is in Peru," Mike said. He handed Grace

the bag of biscuits. "He's a research scientist, like you."

She stilled. "How did you know I'm a research scientist?"

"Arnie told me." Mike glanced at the older man. "Or somebody did."

"No secrets in a small town," Arnie said.

She nodded, said goodbye and returned to her car. Should she text Declan and see if he wanted to get some lunch? But maybe he was busy? She didn't want him to think she had come into town just to see him.

Besides, she had her own work to do. She headed out of town. A glance in the rearview mirror showed a battered green compact car following closely. She didn't think much of it until she turned onto the Forest Service road and the green car followed.

Of course, snowshoers and cross-country skiers used this road to access some of the high-country trails. But she couldn't remember the last time she had seen another car on the road in the middle of a weekday. She looked again in the rearview mirror to see if she recognized the driver, but it was impossible, given tinted windows and the snow that had collected on her rear window.

She focused on negotiating the rough and icy road. No doubt the driver of the green car would turn around before too long, since his vehicle wasn't really made for this kind of driving. Or else he would stop at the parking area for one of the trails.

But they passed the parking area and the green car stayed behind her. Her stomach clenched, but she told herself she was being silly. It was broad daylight, and this was a public roadway. Anyone was allowed to drive it.

She slowed as she approached the sign that announced Road Ends, 100 Feet. Should she stop, or should she turn around? And head back toward the person who followed? Should she wait in her locked vehicle to see what the other driver did?

She decided on the latter. She parked in her usual spot, made sure her doors were locked and waited.

The green car slid to a stop beside her. She still couldn't see the driver clearly, but when the car door opened and he got out, she gasped.

Chapter Thirteen

Tommy, orange knit cap pulled down low over his ears, grinned and waved at her. He stomped through the snow, around her vehicle and up to her driver's side window. "I heard you lived all the way up here, but this is wild!" he said, loud enough to be heard clearly through her closed window.

She hesitated, then lowered the window a few inches. "What are you doing following me?" she asked.

He shoved his hands into the pockets of his parka and looked down. He didn't scuff his feet in a posture of schoolboy humility, but he did look sheepish. "Somebody told me you lived way up in the mountains in an off-grid cabin, and I wanted to see it." He raised his head and met her gaze. "I didn't mean to freak you out. I just think what you're doing is so cool. I'd like to do that, too, one day."

"What happened to your van?" she asked.

When she had seen him at the gas station, he had been driving a van.

He made a face. "It broke down. A friend is letting me use his car until mine is fixed." He looked around. "So where is your cabin? Is it just through there?" He nodded toward the snowmobile trail. "Is that your snowmobile?"

"You need to leave," she said, struggling to keep her voice shaking from a combination of anger and fear. "You had no right to follow me."

"Hey, don't be angry." He took a step back. "I told you I thought it was cool. I know you said you didn't want to go out with me, but I don't see why we can't be friends."

"I don't need any more friends," she said. "Now you really do need to leave."

His smile vanished and his shoulders sagged. "Okay, I'll leave," he said. "Sorry I upset you."

She waited until he turned his car around and had driven out of sight before she made herself get out of her Jeep. Dog treats tucked into one of the pockets of her snowmobile suit, she climbed onto the machine and headed back to the cabin.

Bear's loud barking was a welcome sound. He would let her know if Tommy came back. She loved the dog for many reasons, but one was that he was a good guard dog and his size and bark were intimidating to people who didn't know him.

Inside, she stoked the fire in the woodstove, then paced the floor, heart still racing from her encounter with Tommy. What did he think he was doing, following her to her home? The trouble he had gone to to do so, driving that little car all the way up the rough road, seemed extreme to her.

Fifteen minutes passed before she thought to check her internet and cell service. Everything was back in working order. Before she could talk herself out of it, she punched in Declan's number. When he answered, she almost burst into tears with relief but pulled herself together. "Can you come up to my cabin, please?" she asked. "A man followed me home from town today, and it was really upsetting."

"Who was it?" Declan's voice was sharp with alarm. "Is he there now?"

"He's not here anymore. I told him he had to leave. He's just a guy I met at the gas station. I ran into him again at the library and he asked me out and I turned him down. He wasn't angry or anything. It was just…weird."

"I'll be right there. Don't open the door to anyone or go outside until I get there."

"Don't worry, I won't."

She ended the call, then sat on the sofa, arms

wrapped around herself. She hated this feeling, of being afraid of things that might not even happen.

DECLAN GRIPPED THE steering wheel so hard his knuckles ached, and forced himself to keep his speed down to a safe level to navigate the narrow, snow-packed road. He couldn't help Grace if he ended up stuck in a ditch. He passed no other cars as he climbed, engine growling, toward the trail leading to Grace's cabin, and saw no vehicles parked in the trailhead parking area halfway up the road.

The real fear in her voice when she had called razored through him. *A guy I met at the gas station*, she had said. Was it Barclay? And what about him had made her so afraid?

At last, muscles aching from the tension of holding back, he reached the end of the road. Grace's Jeep sat by itself nearest the snowmobile track to her house. Declan contemplated the long, freezing trek to her cabin and wished he had told her to pick him up on her snowmobile. But that would have meant waiting in the open for him to arrive, vulnerable to Barclay—if her harasser had indeed been Barclay. So Declan zipped his parka up to his chin, put his head down against the wind and began walking.

Her snowmobile sat in front of the cabin. Yellow light glowed in the windows and smoke puffed from the chimney. It looked like something out of a storybook, safe and warm. But as soon as he set his foot on the bottom step leading up to the front porch, furious barking erupted from inside. The curtain at one window fluttered, then the door jerked open and Grace stood there, arms wrapped around herself, looking uncertain.

"Thank you for coming," she said. "I probably overreacted."

"I doubt it." He touched her shoulder briefly, then moved past her, into the warmth of the cabin and Bear's sniffing inspection.

"You must be freezing," Grace said. She took his coat. "Sit down. I've got fresh coffee."

He sat at the end of the sofa closest to the fire and accepted the steaming mug but set it aside to reach for her. "Tell me what happened," he said.

"I was just freaked out that he followed me all the way up here," she said. "He wasn't threatening or anything. It was just so odd. And you told me to be careful of anyone who paid special attention to me."

She was talking too fast, agitated, words tumbling on top of each other as she tried to get all the facts and all the feelings out. "What is his name?" Declan asked, trying to focus on essentials. "Do you know?"

"He said his name is Tommy. He said he's camping in his van somewhere near the river and working at a motel. The Ranch Motel, I think."

Declan felt a cold the fire couldn't touch. "Young guy, thin, little mustache, acne scars," he said.

Grace stared at him. "Yes. How did you know?"

"I gave him a lift to the motel last night. He was walking to town in the cold. He said his van broke down."

"He told me the same thing. He said a friend loaned him a vehicle, a little green compact car."

It was an odd coincidence, both of them interacting with the young man, but not necessarily sinister, not in a community as small as Eagle Mountain.

"What happened, exactly?" he asked.

"My internet was down and I needed to upload a report for work, so I drove to the library to use their computers," she said. "I was almost finished when he sat down at the terminal next to me. We had run into each other a couple of times before around town."

"Where and when?" Declan asked.

"At the gas station, last Saturday," she said.

"And the day Search and Rescue retrieved that mannequin someone put down in the valley, he was there."

"What was he doing there?" Declan asked. Maybe a little too sharply—Grace drew back.

"He was on skis," she said. "It's a public area. Some other skiers who had been there earlier reported seeing a body down in the valley, which turned out to be a mannequin."

"He was by himself?"

She nodded. "I think so. I don't remember anyone else around."

"What did he say then?"

"He said hello and asked what was going on. One of the other rookies, Nancy, told him it was a training exercise. He didn't ask any more questions, and we left."

"Okay. What did he say today, at the library?"

"He asked if I wanted to go out with him for dinner or a drink. I told him no, and he asked if I was married. I said no, I just didn't want to go out. Then he told me he was a fun guy. I was annoyed that he wouldn't drop the idea, so I pretended to be focused on the computer. After a little bit, he got up and wandered off."

"And he followed you home?"

"I didn't drive straight home," she said. "I went to the natural foods store first. I bought some dog biscuits, then I started home. I didn't really notice him until I turned onto the forest road. I noticed this little green car right behind me. I almost never see other cars on this road in winter, so it made me curious. I figured the driver would turn around soon—that little car wasn't really made for these roads. But he kept following, and that made me a little uneasy."

"You should have called me while you still had a signal," he said.

"To tell you another car was behind me on a public road?" She shook her head. "He could have been a sightseer taking a drive or someone planning to snowshoe or ski on a trail."

"But he wasn't either of those things."

"No." She picked up a pillow and hugged it to her stomach. "When I got to the end of the road, he pulled in beside me, so I stayed in my Jeep, with the doors locked. When Tommy got out, I couldn't believe it."

"What did he say that frightened you?"

"I wasn't frightened right away—I was angry. I had told him I didn't want to date him, and he wouldn't take no for an answer. But he didn't get that I was angry. He asked about my cabin and said he had always wanted to live off-grid. I finally told him to leave."

"How did he respond?" Declan asked.

"He acted hurt. But he left. I waited until he was out of sight before I got out of the Jeep and headed out on the snowmobile. When I got here, I found out my phone and cell service were working again, so I called you."

"I'm glad you did," he said. "But if something like this happens again, call the sheriff, too."

"He didn't do anything illegal. He was annoying and clueless, but being awkward isn't a crime."

He hated to admit she was right. Tommy—or Terrence, or whoever he was—hadn't threatened her or even touched her. He left when she asked him to.

Declan took out his phone. "Take a look at this photo and see if the man in it is familiar." He pulled up Terrence Barclay's most recent mug shot and showed it to her.

She frowned at the image. "Is that the man you're looking for?" she asked.

"Just tell me if he looks familiar," Declan said.

"No."

"Look closer. Is there any similarity between him and Tommy?"

She leaned in until her nose was only inches from the phone screen. She studied the photo for a full minute, then shook her head. "They're not the same man, I don't think."

He tucked the phone back into his pocket. He hadn't thought so, either.

"You believe me, don't you?"

The question—and the pain behind it—shocked him. "Of course I believe you," he said. "Why wouldn't I?"

She looked away. "It's nothing."

He touched her cheek and coaxed her to face him again. "It is something, if you're asking."

She curled her hands into fists, then pressed the fists to her cheeks and shook her head. "It's silly," she whispered. A single tear spilled from her right eye and slipped down, over her knuckle and onto the back of her hand.

He pulled her close, wanting to comfort her and wanting to lash out at whatever was causing so much pain. Did she think he wouldn't believe her because he was a cop or because other people didn't believe her? "It's not silly," he said softly. "You're not being silly. Tell me. Who doesn't believe you?"

She pressed her forehead, hard, into his shoulder and shook with silent sobs. Bewildered, he stroked her hair and rubbed her back and waited for the flood to subside. Bear came and rested his chin on her knee, brown eyes full of accusation as he regarded Declan, as if the man was responsible for all this sadness.

Long minutes passed with only the crackle of the fire and the muffled sound of her weeping. Then she fell silent, and he wondered if she was asleep. Her head was heavy and one of his arms was cramping, pinched between her and the back of the sofa, but he wasn't going to move away from her.

Finally, she raised her head and shifted away from him. "Sorry about that," she said. "I haven't broken down like that in a long time."

Which meant she had broken down like that before. The idea made him feel sick. He shifted enough to pull a tissue from his pocket and passed it to her. "Thanks." She blew her nose. "I must look a mess."

"You look beautiful."

She smiled—a brief curve of her lips that made him feel ten feet tall. He clenched his jaw to keep from asking her again to tell him what was wrong. Was this what it felt like to be one of those naturalists who sat for hours outside some wild animal's den, waiting for the timid creature to emerge?

She sat back on the sofa and blew out a breath. "I told you about the accident when I was nine," she said. "The one where I lost my memory."

"Yes."

"I told you my sister died."

"Yes."

She bit her bottom lip, then continued. "I didn't tell you that I was the one who caused the accident. I was the reason she died. The reason my mom and I were hurt, the reason the car was destroyed."

"No," he said. "You were nine. And how do you know it was your fault? You can't remember."

"I know because my mom told me." Her eyes met his, and his anger rose in the face of her misery. "She told me all the time that my sister would have lived if I hadn't been so bad that day."

He took her hand and squeezed but said nothing. He thought she might start crying again, but she sat up a little straighter and continued. "Mom was driving us to my swimming lesson. I was excited because we were supposed to dive off the high dive that day. I was in the back seat and my sister, Hope, was buckled into her car seat next to me. Mom told me I wouldn't be still. I unbuckled my seat belt, then I undid the buckle on Hope's car seat, even though Mom told me not to. She was half-turned to yell at me when the car went off the road and rolled. Hope was thrown from the car on impact and I was hurt badly, too. Much worse than if we had been buckled in." She shook her head. "Mom never forgave me. I'm sure she wanted to, but how could she? She drank more and more after that. She always managed to keep a job, but she would come home from work and drink until she passed out. She died of liver failure while I was still in college. So I guess you could say I killed her, too."

"You were a child," Declan said. "It was wrong of her to blame you. And wrong of you to blame yourself."

"I was a child, but I knew better," she said. "I was old enough to know better."

"Where was this?" he asked. "When?"

"A little town called Simpson, Iowa. July, more than twenty years ago."

"A long time ago, and a long way away from here." He tried to pull her close, but she leaned away.

"I understand if you want to go now," she said.

"I'm not going anywhere," he said. "I'm not going to leave you by yourself." Not when she was drowning in this old pain.

"I killed my baby sister and my mother," she said. "Why would you want to have anything to do with me?"

"It was an accident," he said. "It's not the same. And you were a child. You're a woman now, and you're not a killer. No more than I am."

"How could this not change how you think about me?" She stared at him, searching his face, as if for some indication that he was lying.

"It doesn't change things because I love you."

The truth of those words, spoken out loud, hit him with the force of an avalanche. He struggled for a second to catch his breath, aware of his heart racing and a lump in his throat.

"You don't really know me," she said, but the harshness was gone from her voice, replaced with wonder.

"I think I do." He swallowed past the lump. "I know the woman who saved my life, who volunteers to save other lives. I know someone who had the strength to push past a great tragedy to make a life for herself and do important work that will help generations to come. I know that you're smart and you're kind—and you make me feel things I didn't think I was capable of feeling."

That quirk of a smile again and that same melting feeling inside his chest. "Don't tell me you've never been in love," she said.

"I've been in lust. I've been infatuated. But I'm pretty sure some wise person once said in order to love, you have to love yourself first. You're not the only one who grew up hearing you didn't measure up."

"Your father," she said.

He nodded. "I wasn't the general's idea of a perfect son, though I doubt such a paragon exists. I thought I'd found my place in the Marshals Service, where I did a good job and was

rewarded for it. I excelled even, until I didn't."
A familiar tightness in his shoulders—he fought
against it. "It doesn't matter how old you are
or how successful you are, there are situations
where you are five or ten or fifteen, being lec-
tured on how much you disappointed someone
who was counting on you. My supervisor at the
Marshals Service was saying the words, but all
I heard was my dad."

"Oh, Declan." She leaned into him again, and
they held each other, eyes closed, fire crackling,
letting the silence be a balm for the pain.

Chapter Fourteen

All the old scripts tried to play out again in Grace's head, from the one about how selfish she was, never thinking of anyone else, to the one about her being born bad, with a nasty streak that made her impossible to love. She had had enough therapy over the years to acknowledge these were lies, but really believing they were wrong took more work on some days than others.

And here was Declan, the victim of his own parental lies. Except she was sure he had never failed as spectacularly as she had. He had never contributed to the death of an innocent baby and the destruction of a family.

But he said he loved her, anyway. What a miracle that was. It made her believe that the feelings she had for him might be real and not merely wishful thinking.

Today. Right now, at least, she wasn't going to allow doubt to tarnish the moment. She shifted against him and kissed the sharp edge of his jaw, then moved to his lips—firm and warm and exactly what she wanted. He slid one hand beneath her hair and cradled her head and returned the kiss with such fierceness she knew he needed this closeness as much as she did.

"Can you stay the night?" she asked.

"I intend to," he said.

"Then let's go into the bedroom."

Would it always be this intense for them? she wondered as they began to undress each other. As if they feared the moment might slip away if they didn't rush to capture it. Or as if they couldn't contain all the emotion behind every movement.

He lifted her sweater over her head, then paused to kiss her shoulder, his mouth hot against her skin, sending tremors through her. She arched her neck as he pressed his lips to the pulse at the base of her throat, and she imagined her heartbeat becoming a part of him.

When they were both naked, she led him to the bed. He retrieved the condom from the bedside table this time and arranged the pillows and blankets so they would both be more comfortable. As if he planned for them to stay awhile.

"What are you smiling about?" he asked.

She hadn't even realized she was smiling. "I'm just happy," she said.

"I want to make you happy." He lay back and pulled her on top of him, and she gave herself up to exploring him, the way she might examine an as-yet-undiscovered mountain valley. She shivered as she skimmed her hands across the crisp curls on his chest and felt the heat rise in her as she traced the ridges of his abdomen. When she dipped her head to the juncture of his thighs, he groaned and threaded his fingers through her hair, as if he needed that hold to weight him to the earth.

They took turns on these journeys of discovery, trading places on the bed, letting fingers and mouths reveal all the outer mysteries, now that they had shared so much of their inner secrets. When they came together at last, she had never felt closer to anyone. Was it love or merely strong passion that allowed her to lose herself so fully?

And then she stopped thinking altogether, focused only on physical sensation, tension pulling tighter and tighter until she let go, falling and falling, only to land safely in his arms.

"You were smiling again," he whispered, his mouth close to her ear.

"Mmm." She wrapped her legs more tightly around him. "Better hurry and catch up," she said, and so he did.

DECLAN RELUCTANTLY LEFT Grace the next morning. What they had between them felt too fragile to push for too much. He wanted to give Grace plenty of space, and he welcomed a little time to process things himself.

First, there was the childhood tragedy Grace had revealed and the enormous burden she had carried all these years. It was just as well her mother was no longer around—if Declan had ever met her, he didn't know if he could have stopped himself from berating her for the cruel way she had treated her daughter.

He tried to picture Grace at nine—small and thin or short and sturdy, no sign of the woman to come in her body. Had she loved her little sister or been jealous of her? But would she really have unfastened the child's car seat? Why do so? To play with her? He hadn't been around children enough to know if that was something they would do or not.

But it didn't matter. Even if Grace had unbuckled her sister and distracted her mother, she'd been a child. How could a mother not see that?

He knew he wouldn't get anywhere, running that sad story over and over in his mind, so he turned his attention to the chief reason he was in Eagle Mountain: Terrence Barclay.

He started at the sheriff's department, where he caught Gage as the sergeant was headed out the door. "We need to talk," Declan said.

"Something happened to Grace yesterday afternoon that you should know about."

Gage led the way back to his office. "Is Grace all right?" he asked.

"She was pretty shaken up, but she's all right now." Declan settled into the visitor's chair. "Do you know a guy named Tommy? Lives in a van by the river and works nights at the Ranch Motel."

"I know who you're talking about," Gage said. "What about him?"

"He followed Grace up to her cabin yesterday afternoon," Declan said. "Or almost to the cabin. He drove up to the end of the Forest Service road. Apparently, he saw her in the library and asked her out, but she turned him down."

"Did he threaten her or try to harm her?" Gage asked.

"She says no, but she called me, clearly upset by it all. He said he wanted to see where she lived. She told him to leave, and he finally did." He gripped the arms of the chair and leaned toward Gage. "What if Tommy is really Terrence Barclay and he's fixated on Grace as his next victim? He's the right age, he just moved to town and he's following Barclay's pattern of taking a temporary job while he's here."

Gage turned to his computer. "Do you have a last name?"

"Llewellyn."

"Let's see what we can find." Gage began typing. "I'll try Thomas and Tom, too." He scanned the list of names, then typed some more. "I think I've found him." He slid the chair back and angled the monitor to show a mug shot, clean-shaven with the hair a little shorter. Mug shots were notoriously unflattering, but Declan thought this was the same man he had driven to the motel two nights before.

"What does his sheet say?" Declan asked.

"Petty stuff," Gage said. "Shoplifting. Possession. He did six months in the Larimer County jail for breaking and entering." He scrolled some more. "Looks like he was released about two months ago. If this is the same guy, he's not Terrence Barclay."

"No," Declan conceded. "But what was he doing, frightening Grace?"

Gage slid his chair back. "Let's go ask him."

Declan rose also.

"You can come with me," Gage said, "but don't say anything. I'd like for you to get a good look at this guy and confirm that he isn't Barclay."

Declan didn't volunteer that he had already spent a good half hour in a car with Llewellyn and nothing about him had seemed familiar.

He rode in the passenger seat of Gage's department-issue SUV, after moving aside a file box, a leather coat, a pair of headphones and a half box of ammunition. "I was out at the shooting range yesterday afternoon," Gage said by way of explanation.

"Do you know where Llewellyn is camping?" Declan asked as Gage drove out of town.

"I've got a pretty good idea," Gage said. "There are a couple of popular places, though usually no one uses them this time of year."

"It would get awfully cold in a van at night," Declan said.

"Maybe that's why Llewellyn works the night shift at the motel—to stay warmer."

Maybe, Declan agreed. Though for someone trying to stay out of the public eye, the night shift was a good choice, too.

"I'm curious why Grace contacted you about this instead of the sheriff's department," Gage said.

"She was frightened, but Llewellyn talked to her on public land," Declan said. "He didn't lay a hand on her, and he wasn't even trespassing. I don't think most people would have called the sheriff's department."

"But she called you. I take it the two of you have stayed in touch."

"Do you have a problem with that?"

"No. I'm just nosy." Gage grinned. "And I've

always been curious about Grace. There aren't many young women who would choose to live so isolated. I remember seeing her a few times in the summers, when she would come to stay with her grandfather."

"You grew up here?" Declan asked.

"Travis and I grew up on a ranch outside of town, but we spent plenty of time in town, playing baseball, going to church camp, things like that. We ran into Grace a few times."

"What was she like?"

"Quiet. I don't think she ever said a word to me, though I tried to get her attention. We all wondered about her, partly because she was from somewhere else, but mostly because she lived with a man we called the Hermit of the Hills. We made up scary stories about the old man, like he killed trespassers and buried them in his backyard, or he had a hidden stash of gold he was guarding. Silly kid stuff."

"Grace says she loved spending summers with him. She didn't want to leave, but she had to return to school."

"I've read a few articles about the work he did in that cabin," Gage said. "He was way ahead of his time, studying the climate and natural history. We've had scientists from all over the world who have traveled here to see him or to study his records. It's nice that Grace is able to carry on his work, but it's not a life everyone would choose."

Declan started to say that Grace was happy, but was she? How could she be, when she carried such deep sadness inside of her over a childhood tragedy she couldn't even remember?

Gage turned onto a narrow Forest Service road, guiding his SUV through icy ruts. After about a mile, they spotted a faded red van parked on the right side of the road. "I think this is the place," Gage said. He pulled in behind the van and sat for a moment with the engine running. "I'm going to run the plate," he said and began typing into the laptop mounted between the seats.

"It comes back registered to Bernard Gross," he said. "Gross died six months ago and the van's not listed as stolen. Maybe he was a relative?"

The door to the van opened and Llewellyn, dressed in gray sweats and house slippers, stepped out and frowned in their direction.

"Let's see what he has to say," Gage said and opened the door.

Declan followed, automatically taking up a defensive position a few steps behind and to one side, his gaze fixed on Llewellyn's hands, but the young man made no suspicious moves. "Hello, Deputy," he said and nodded to Gage.

"Tommy Llewellyn?" Gage asked.

"Yes, sir. Is there something wrong? I was told it was okay to camp here, on public land."

"We wanted to talk to you about a young woman you followed home yesterday afternoon," Gage said. "Apparently you asked her out and wouldn't take no for an answer."

"Aw, man, it wasn't like that." He held out both hands in a pleading gesture. "I mean, yeah, I asked her out. I liked her. She was nice to me."

"Just because someone is nice to you doesn't give you permission to harass them." So much for Declan's pledge not to say anything. Gage glared at him.

"I wasn't harassing her, truly." Llewellyn looked stricken. "I just… I followed her because I had heard she lived in this cabin up in the mountains, off-grid and everything. It sounded so cool. I just wanted to see it. I just wanted to be friends." He looked from Gage to Declan, then stared hard at Declan. "Hey, you're the guy who gave me a lift to work the other night. I didn't know you were a cop."

Another hard look from Gage, which Declan ignored.

Gage turned back to Llewellyn. "Can you understand how a woman would be frightened by a man who followed her from town all the way to her home?" he asked.

"I guess so, but I didn't mean it that way. Honest!" He wiped a hand across his mouth and looked stricken. "I'm not in trouble, am I? I don't want to cause anyone trouble. You probably already know I've got a record, but I did my time and I'm staying out of trouble. I have a job and everything. I don't want to bother anybody."

"Do yourself a favor and stay away from Grace," Gage said. "And the next time you want to be friends with a woman, don't follow her around if she tells you no."

"I won't," Llewellyn said. "I promise."

Gage nodded. "You have a good day."

Declan followed Gage back to the SUV. They drove past Llewellyn, turned around and headed back to town. "You didn't tell me you knew him," Gage said.

"I don't know him," Declan said. "I gave him a ride to work after I picked him up walking on the side of the road on a freezing cold night. It was dark and I didn't get that good a look at him."

"What do you think—does he look like Barclay?"

"He didn't look familiar, but that doesn't mean a lot when it comes to Barclay," Declan said. "Plenty of people who know him a lot better than I do have failed to recognize him."

"And they weren't hit on the head and dealing with memory loss," Gage said.

Declan didn't reply.

"My take is he really liked Grace and went about trying to be friends in the wrong way," Gage said. "There's no malice behind it."

"People thought Barclay was harmless, too," Declan said. He sighed. "But you're right. Llewellyn struck me as more pathetic than anything."

"I know you've been talking to people around town," Gage said. "Is there anyone else we need to take a closer look at?"

He appreciated Gage wasn't merely dismissing him. "Most of the businesses I've talked to haven't hired many people lately," he said. "They're waiting for the summer tourist season. One guy I found was way too short to be Barclay, and another turned out to be from here originally and had just moved back to town. I found his picture in a high school yearbook at the library, so that checked out. The only other person on my list is Mike—the guy we saw in Mo's Pub the other day."

"He said he's the son of a friend of Arnie's, who runs the natural foods store," Gage said.

"Yeah, but we only have his word for that."

"Then let's have a word with Arnie."

Ten minutes later, Gage parked in front of a

simple storefront with the sign Natural Foods. "How long has this place been here?" Declan asked.

"Three or four years," Gage said. "This used to be a house."

A leather harness festooned with old-fashioned sleigh bells jangled as they opened the door, and their footsteps echoed on the worn wooden floors. A stout man with bald spot above a rim of graying brown curls looked up from behind the counter. "Hello, Gage," he said. "What can I do for you today?"

"Hey, Arnie." Gage walked to the counter. "How's it going?"

While the two of them made small talk, Declan assessed the place. It reminded him of an old-fashioned general store, with products displayed on racks of plain wooden shelves or in deep baskets. Red-checked curtains flanked the windows, and framed photographs filled the walls. On closer inspection, these proved to be a younger version of Arnie engaged in various adventures. Declan paused in front of a photo of a quartet of men in heavy parkas gathered around a small plane in an icy landscape.

"That was taken at the Amundsen-Scott research station at the South Pole." Arnie came to stand beside Declan. "That's me in the middle." He pointed a stubby finger at the shortest of the trio, his thick mustache frosted with ice. A notation in pen in the photo's bottom margin identified the mustached man as Arnie Cowdrey.

"What were you doing at the South Pole?" Declan asked.

"Geological surveying," Arnie said. "I was there for six months right out of college. Terrific adventure." He moved over to a second picture with the same group of men, this time sprawled on sofas in a room crowded with bookshelves and cardboard boxes. Arnie wore a lumberjack checked shirt and a knit cap "There were a group of us young guys who hung out. In our off time, we played a lot of video games and watched a lot of TV," Arnie said.

"Is that where you knew Mike's dad?" Gage asked.

Arnie looked over his shoulder at Gage. "You know Mike?"

"I met him in Mo's the other day," Gage said. "He told me he was working for you."

Arnie nodded. "That's his dad right there." He stabbed his finger at the person posed next to him in the photo, a tall, thin man with thick brown hair and the beginnings of a beard. "Mickey Randolph. Terrific guy."

"That was good of you to take on his son," Gage said.

Arnie waved away the praise. "The kid came

in here and said his dad told him to look me up and say hello. But it didn't take long to find out he was desperate to find work and settle down. He said he'd gotten in a little trouble back home and was trying to get his life back on track. Hey, I was young once. I know what it's like to do something foolish. I'd been thinking I could use some help here, so it worked out well all around. He's doing a great job for me."

"That's good to hear," Gage said. He met Declan's gaze over the top of Arnie's head and shook his head slightly. They weren't going to find anything here.

"It's been fun having the kid around," Arnie said. "He reminds me a lot of his old man." He tapped the photo.

Declan studied the image again. Did Mike look like the man in the photo? They both had dark hair, but beyond that, it was impossible to tell. The faces in the photo were no bigger than Declan's thumb, faded and blurred with time.

Arnie moved back to the counter. "Is that why you stopped in—to talk about Mike?"

"Actually, I need some more of that ginger lemonade you sell." Gage walked toward a cooler in the back. "Maya says it's the only thing that settles her stomach right now."

"We'll fix her up," Arnie said. "And tell her I

have some ginger chews she can try, too. Some women swear by them."

Gage paid for his purchase and stowed it in the SUV. "My wife is pregnant," he said by way of explanation.

"Your first?" Declan asked.

"Her first pregnancy, but we adopted her niece. Casey is seven now. She's a great kid."

What would that be like, Declan wondered, not for the first time, to have a family who depended on you? Would it make it harder to put on a weapon and a ballistics vest and put your life on the line every day? Or would you feel the work you did was even more important?

They got back into the SUV and Gage started the engine, but he didn't drive away. "Do you still think Terrence Barclay is here in Eagle Mountain?" he asked.

"Yes."

"Because he killed Agnes Cockrell and he won't leave until he's planned and carried out the murder of another woman," Gage said.

"Yes. That's the pattern he's followed twice that we know of, but probably all three times, in three different places," he said.

"What if he's decided to break pattern?" Gage asked. "What if he dumped Agnes's car in Delta, stole another vehicle there and headed to Utah or farther west?"

"Have there been killings in those areas that might be linked to Barclay?" Declan asked. "Have you checked?"

"I've checked," Gage said. "I didn't spot anything, but maybe it hasn't shown up in any databases or made the news."

"Why would he break that pattern now?" Declan said. "I'm not an expert, but it seems from what I've read that something traumatic would need to happen to cause a break in the pattern. Killers like this seem to fixate on behaving in certain ways. It's often how they're caught—because they can't break the pattern even if they would be better off if they did."

"So if he didn't break the pattern and he is here, what happens next?" Gage asked.

"He's probably picked out his next victim and is watching her, planning to make his move," Declan said.

"That's why you freaked out when Llewellyn followed Grace."

"Yes." He swallowed down the remnants of that fear from when he had thought she might have come to Barclay's attention. "But he might not be so obvious as to follow the woman. It could be someone he works with, who he sees every day. Or someone who lives near him. She probably doesn't realize she's caught his attention."

"We could use some help trying to find him," Gage said.

"We could," Declan agreed. "But I don't know if we're going to get any. I talked to my boss. The marshals and the FBI don't think Barclay is here. They're not sending anyone to look for him."

"Then I guess it's up to us."

One disgraced US deputy marshal and a small-town sheriff's department against a man who had eluded scores of law enforcement for a number of local and federal agencies. His father had always chided him for taking on what he termed foolish risks. Why change his approach now?

Chapter Fifteen

Grace was on the phone with Declan when she received a text from Search and Rescue. "I guess you won't be coming up to see me tonight," she said after she read the text. "I need to help search for a missing skier."

"Would you call me when you get in so I know you're all right?" he asked. "It doesn't matter how late."

"I will." She realized she was smiling when she hung up the phone. Who knew having someone to worry about you would feel so good?

But she didn't have time to savor the feeling. She hurried to change clothes, fed Bear, then gathered her gear and headed to her Jeep for the trip to Search and Rescue headquarters.

"We've got a seventy-year-old man who was skiing by himself and failed to return home for dinner," Sheri told the assembled volunteers half an hour later. "Eddie Pearlman."

A murmur went through the group at the

name. "Eddie is an experienced skier," Danny Irwin said. "He knows all the local trails."

"According to his wife, he planned to ski one of the trails at Alexander Basin. He left the house at 10:00 a.m. and thought he would be home by four." She checked her watch. "He's almost three hours overdue. We'll divide up in teams to search the trails. Watch for tracks, but there was heavy snow in the higher elevations around noon, so it's possible his tracks will have been covered over."

At the trailhead, Grace clicked into her skis. She was paired with Eldon Ramsey, and they headed up Sharp Shin Trail. The earlier clouds had cleared, and the night was cold and still, the Milky Way a wide ribbon of glitter overhead. Grace quickly found a rhythm and glided along, skis buoyant in the deep snow. She was comfortable on skis, having covered miles with her grandfather, checking animal dens and stands of aspen, photographing, measuring or merely sitting quietly, waiting for the animals to emerge. If you were very still and waited long enough, they would go about their normal activities, unspooked by your presence.

Her grandfather had taught her the healing power of solitude and the natural world. Nothing there would judge her or condemn her. Animals and trees didn't look at time linearly, her grandfather had explained. For them, there was only now. They collected food for the winter because instinct told them to do so now, not because they feared the future.

She wasn't certain her grandfather had been right about that, but the idea intrigued her. Not that she wanted to live never looking back on good memories or anticipating pleasant times ahead. But it would be good to let go of the terrible things in the past and to be able to face the future without fear.

"Have you skied these trails before?" Eldon asked. She didn't know the big man well, except that he was originally from Hawaii and he worked for the biggest gold mine in the area. He was acknowledged as one of the physically strongest members of the team, an accomplished climber and skier with a cheerful outlook.

"A few times," she said. "What about you?"

He shook his head. "I mostly do downhill skiing, but this is pretty interesting." He stopped and pointed to a set of small animal tracks, each toe and segment of paw clearly outlined in the snow. "I never realized you could see so much out here. What do you think they are?"

She studied the tracks. "Probably an ermine," she said. "A long-tailed weasel's tracks would be farther apart."

He grinned at her. "We don't have those in

Hawaii. I'm still learning the local wildlife and plants. It's interesting stuff."

"It is," she agreed.

"You should take the lead," he said and motioned for her to move past him. "You're obviously a better skier."

She moved past him but stayed close enough to continue their conversation. "Do you know the man we're looking for?" she asked.

"I never met him, but I know about him," Eldon said. "He heads up the local historical society, leads hikes to mine ruins in the summer and gives slideshows about mine history. Some of these old guys can hike rings around me."

"My grandfather skied and hiked right up to the day before he died, when he was eighty-six," Grace said. "I've got logs that showed him skiing one hundred miles or more in a week. He never had a snowmobile while he was living here—if he needed to go somewhere, he went on skis."

"If your grandfather had gotten hurt, what would he have done?" Eldon asked.

She considered the question. "When I was a girl, he told me if I ever got hurt when I was out alone, I should stay put for at least the first twenty-four to thirty-six hours. He told me to build a fire if I could, but if I couldn't do that and it was winter, to scrape out a snow cave.

Burrow in like the mink or weasel and wait for help. If help didn't show up by the second day, then I was supposed to start moving, but only if I could keep track of where I was going. He told me to travel from one known landmark to the next. He said if I didn't know where I was, I should stop and wait."

Her voice broke and she cleared her throat and faced forward to blink away sudden, stinging tears. She hadn't thought of that conversation with her grandfather in years, but remembering it now, she was struck by how much he had cared for her. "Pay attention," he had said that day. "I don't want anything bad to happen to you." How could she have forgotten that?

"That all makes a lot of sense," Eldon said. He looked around them, the beam of his headlamp illuminating dark evergreens and sparkling snow. "So let's say you're Eddie Pearlman. If he had a heart attack, he would have keeled over right on the trail and we would have found him by now. But let's say instead he fell and hurt himself—maybe he got off the trail in some deep snow." He sniffed. "I don't smell any smoke, so he probably didn't build a fire. But a snow cave—let's look for something like that."

"It would be off the trail a bit," she said, trying to picture it. "But what would it look like?"

"A mound of snow?" He looked around at the

uneven terrain. "Maybe with disturbed ground around, where he had raked up the snow. It's not going to be easy to see, but it's something to watch for."

She nodded, then cupped her hands to her mouth and shouted. "Eddie! Eddie, are you okay?"

No response but her own pulse, thudding in her ears. "Come on," Eldon said. "Let's keep going. We're not going to give up yet."

Grace and Eldon continued down the trail for another mile, scanning either side. The head-lamps cast a weak beam only a short distance into the woods, and starlight provided little illumination in the thick cover. They paused every few minutes to shout for Eddie and listen for a reply, but only a complaint from an aggrieved owl nearby answered. The cold had seeped through Grace's clothing until her fingers and toes ached, and she was wondering how much longer they could continue to search when her light swept across an odd shape to the right of the trail.

She stopped and focused more closely on what appeared to be a pile of evergreen branches, dusted with snow.

"Why are you stopping?" Eldon asked.

"Those branches over there." She pointed. "I remember something else my grandfather told me. He said if I was hurt or lost during the summer, I should gather branches to make a shelter. Maybe that's what Eddie did. If he couldn't dig in the snow, he could drag branches into a pile to make a kind of shelter."

"It does look out of place," Eldon said. "Let's check it out." He used his pole to click out of his skis, and she did the same. She sank almost to her knees in snow as soon as she stepped off the trail, but there were too many downed tree trunks and protruding boulders here to make navigating on skis possible.

She let Eldon break trail toward the pile of snow-covered branches. "Eddie!" he shouted. "Eddie Pearlman! Are you all right?"

"Help! Over here!"

Eldon took off running, and Grace stumbled after him. They found Eddie Pearlman lying in a tunnel of branches, one leg held awkwardly to his side. "I think I broke my leg," he said. "I figured I'd wait out the night here and try to crawl back to the trail in the morning."

"You don't have to do that now," Eldon said and pulled out his radio to contact Sheri and the others.

Within half an hour, four volunteers had arrived with a litter. Danny Irwin administered pain medication and stabilized the injured leg while Grace and Hannah placed warming packs around Eddie and blankets over him. They gave him water and an energy gel and carefully loaded him onto the litter for the trip out to the trailhead, where an ambulance waited.

Eldon helped carry the litter while Grace followed. Sheri met them at the trailhead. "Good work, you two," she said and clapped them both on the back.

"Grace deserves all the credit," Eldon said. "She's the one who thought to look for some kind of shelter, and she spotted the pile of branches Eddie was under."

"I was just remembering what my grandfather taught me," she said. "Eldon asked the right questions to make me think of it. I'm glad Eddie is okay."

"He's going to be fine," Hannah said.

Everyone took turns congratulating Grace. By the time she left headquarters, she felt as if she was floating, she was so happy.

She was also hungry. Maybe she would treat herself to pizza. No one delivered to where she lived, and anything she got to-go would be ice-cold by the time she got back to the cabin.

She remembered her promise to call Declan. "Hey," he answered. "How's it going?"

"Good. We found the skier, and he's going to be all right."

"That's great. Where are you now?"

"I'm still in town, and I'm starving. Want to meet me at Mo's and get pizza? I know it's late, but—"

"I'll be there in five minutes."

IT WAS CLOSER to ten minutes, but Declan met her in front of the pub and soon they were seated at a table by the front window, awaiting an order of a pepperoni-and-mushroom pizza. She was telling him the story of their discovery of Eddie Pearlman when she was distracted by something behind him. She stopped speaking and stared over his shoulder.

"What is it?" Declan started to turn around, but she put a hand on his arm.

"It's just the guy who works at the natural foods store," she said. "Why is he glaring at you?"

Declan turned to look, in time to see Mike moving toward the bar.

"Do you know him?" Grace asked.

"Not really." He sipped from the beer he had ordered. "He's probably angry that I was asking his boss questions about him."

"He's the son of a friend of Arnie's."

"So I heard. I just wanted to make sure that was true."

"Why wouldn't it be true?"

"Because people don't always tell the truth."

"Are you always this cynical?"

"Being a cop makes me more suspicious, I guess."

She stiffened. "Are you suspicious of me?"

He had upset her, and that was the last thing he wanted to do. "No." He took her hand in his and caressed it. "You know I'm still looking for Terrence Barclay. He's good at disguising himself, so I'm checking out everyone who could be him."

"Do you mean like Tommy?"

"Has he bothered you anymore?" he asked.

She shook her head. "No. I haven't seen or heard anything from him. But do you think—"

"No. Gage and I checked him out. He's not Barclay. And I don't think he meant you any harm. He's just clueless."

She relaxed a little. "I feel bad now, like maybe I overreacted," she said.

"Pepperoni-and-mushroom pizza?" A server slid the pizza pan between them. "You two need anything else?"

"Thanks," Declan said. "We're good." As soon as the server was gone, he turned back to Grace. "Don't feel bad. He had no right to follow you that way. You live by yourself in a remote location. It's good that you're careful."

She slid a slice of pizza onto her plate. "I've never been afraid up there before," she said. "It was the one place where I always felt safest. I was thinking today about how nothing in nature judges you or cares about what you did in the past."

"I don't judge you or care about what you did in the past."

She met his gaze, and the sadness in her eyes made him hurt. He would do anything to remove that sadness. He turned the conversation back to that night's search and her triumph in finding Eddie Pearlman.

"It felt really good," she admitted. "It's why I joined Search and Rescue. To truly help people. All the training has been interesting and the other volunteers have really welcomed me, but tonight was the first time I really felt like part of something bigger."

They finished their pizza, and while they waited for the check, he took her hand. "Will you come back to the Alpiner with me?" he asked.

"You know my friend Hannah works and lives there, right? It's going to be awkward if she sees me going up to your room. I mean, is the rate different for two people? Do I have to register? And I can't leave Bear locked in the cabin all night."

"It's okay," he said, hiding his disappointment.

"You know I want to be with you, right?" she said. "I'm not ashamed or anything like that."

"Even if I'm a cynical cop?" He smiled to take the sting from the words.

"It's probably a good thing for a cop to be cynical," she said. "It's just, this is a small town and everyone talks about everyone else."

"And you're a private person who likes to keep things to yourself," he said.

She nodded. "Yes."

He leaned closer and spoke more softly. "Then what if I come back to the cabin with you?"

Heat sparked in her eyes. "That would be great."

He paid the check, helped her with her coat and they walked out. The plan was for him to follow her up to her place.

As he was walking to his truck, he passed Mike Randolph, standing at the entrance to the alley beside the pub, smoking a cigarette. Declan nodded in greeting, but Mike turned away. Guess he had made an enemy there. But that was nothing new. Another thing about being a cop he hadn't shared with Grace: your real friends were few and far between.

Chapter Sixteen

Grace lay awake that night, long after Declan had fallen asleep. What Declan said about being suspicious of everyone had stuck with her. He didn't trust people. He naturally thought the worst of them. He had said that didn't apply to her, but if that was his nature, how could he help himself? Maybe right now, in the first rush of emotion between them, he thought she was wonderful, but what happened later, when life wore the shine off their relationship? She had confessed to him that she had done something terrible. Something unforgivable. How could that not tarnish every aspect of her life, including his feelings for her?

Even her grandfather, who had loved her more than anyone in the world, had believed she wasn't like other people. She shuddered as she thought back to a conversation she had overheard in this very cabin, when she was thirteen or fourteen. Her mother had arrived to take her back to Iowa for the school year. She had been sent to her bedroom in the loft to gather her things, but she had returned in time to hear her mother say, "The older she gets, the harder she is for me to deal with. I've never met a more sullen child, or one so deliberately contrary."

"She doesn't behave that way for me," her grandfather had said.

"Only because you spoil her. And because you haven't been around children enough to know what's normal and what's not."

"Grace is different," her grandfather had said. "I think everything she's been through has damaged more than her memory."

Grace had hurried back to her room then, not wanting to hear more. Her grandfather thought she was damaged—broken. Unable to be repaired. Declan would learn that about her soon enough.

She rolled over and squeezed her eyes shut, trying to cry without making a sound. She didn't think she would sleep, but she must have, because when she woke, Declan's side of the bed was empty.

She found him stoking the fire in the woodstove. He looked up and smiled at her. He had showered, the ends of his hair still damp, and she caught the clean, herbal smell of the shaving cream he had borrowed.

"Good morning, sleepyhead," he said. "I made coffee."

"Thanks." She headed for the kitchen, ignoring her first instinct, which was to kiss him, to linger in his warm embrace, maybe even suggest they both head back to bed. Instead, she poured a mug of coffee and stood staring out the kitchen window at the glittering white world.

He moved in behind her and wrapped his arms around her. "What say I make some breakfast?" he asked. "You have everything here for pancakes."

"I really need to get to work." She moved out of his embrace, as far away as the small room would let her, which was only a few feet. "I think you should probably go."

Suddenly, the room was several degrees colder. She couldn't look at him, but she felt the chill and the new stiffness in his body. "What's wrong?" he asked.

She shook her head. She owed him an explanation, but how to explain? "I know you're going back to Denver soon," she said. "To your job and your old life. And my life is here. It's been great, but what we have between us, it isn't sustainable."

"What do you mean it isn't sustainable? Denver is only six hours from here. We have phones and cars. It's not like we'll never see each other."

"You don't need to feel obligated just because I pulled you out of that blizzard. Anyone would have done the same."

"I'm not with you because I feel obligated." His voice rose, real anger behind the words. "Grace, what is going on? Last night everything was fine between us. Better than fine. And this morning you're sending me away like I've done something to hurt you."

She forced herself to look him in the eye. She owed him that much. "You haven't hurt me," she said. "You've been wonderful. But you will hurt me one day. You won't be able to help it. The two of us look at the world in completely different ways, and it isn't going to work out between us. Not for the long haul. I'd rather end this now, before we're in any deeper."

"I love you," he said. "Didn't you hear me say that?"

"You think you love me. But you don't even know me."

"I know that I connect with you in a way I've never connected with anyone before. It doesn't matter that we've only known each other a couple of weeks. I know you. And you know me."

She shook her head, feeling the tears threatening. She was weakening, and that wasn't a good thing. "Please leave," she said. "Please."

He stood still for so long she began to wonder what she would do if he simply refused to go. Would she have to leave the cabin and not come back until it was empty again?

But finally, he exited the room. She followed the sound of his footsteps as he went into the bedroom, then emerged to linger by the kitchen door for a long minute. She stared at the floor, refusing to look at him again until he left, out the door this time. He would have a long, cold walk to his truck, but that couldn't be helped. Maybe the fact that she had forced him to make that walk would anger him enough that he would stay away.

When she was sure he was gone, she sank to her knees on the kitchen floor. Bear came over to her, and she buried her face in the soft fur of his neck and cried and cried.

DECLAN SCARCELY FELT the cold on the walk back to his truck. He was too angry, hurt and confused to notice any physical sensation. What had prompted Grace's complete change of heart? He could think of nothing he had said or done to set her off this way. She had seemed enthusiastic about the prospect of him spending the night at her house last night, and their lovemaking had been as passionate and tender as ever. As he'd lain beside her before he'd drifted to sleep, he couldn't remember ever being happier.

He replayed the conversation with her over in his head. No, she wasn't angry at him. She was sad. Hurt. But not hurt by him. He had taken enough psychology courses as part of his law enforcement training to recognize that. He didn't even have to ask himself what had hurt her because she had told him herself. Her whole life had been built around the auto accident when she was nine and its aftermath: the death of her sister, her own injuries and resultant amnesia, the blame her mother placed on her for everything that happened.

Grace had said she wanted to end her relationship with him now because it would hurt less than waiting until later. She was sure he would fall out of love with her, but why?

Because she believed he would eventually blame her for what had happened to her sister? That was impossible. Or maybe she thought he would fall out of love with her because she didn't deserve love?

The idea she would think that made him want to shout with anger. It also made him feel utterly helpless. Because if that was what Grace believed, what could he do about it? He could urge her to see a therapist. He could tell her every day that she deserved love. He could try to show her.

But he couldn't fight the beliefs people had

about themselves, whether he was up against a serial killer or the woman he loved.

He wasn't the type of person who could remain passive. His whole life had been spent around doing, from the tasks his father set in which Declan tried to prove himself to his job in law enforcement. As a marshal, he had work to do all day, whether it was transporting a prisoner or tracking down a fugitive. He had to use his brain as well as his body to do these things, but there were always lists of actions he could take. A lawman didn't sit behind a desk and wait for criminals to come to him.

Back at the Alpiner, Declan booted up his computer and turned to what he knew best—the task of researching and strategizing and taking action to solve a problem.

He logged into a newspaper database and was able to pull up the issue of the Simpson, Iowa, *Sentinel* for the time of Grace's car accident. He might have expected the story he was looking for to be on the front page, but he had to scroll through several pages before he found it: one car accident resulting in one fatality.

The facts were pretty much as Grace had stated. Thirty-six-year-old Jennifer Wilcox had lost control of her Chevrolet Cobalt. The car had left the road and rolled once before slamming into a tree. Wilcox's three-year-old daughter was thrown from the vehicle and died as a result. Her nine-year-old daughter suffered a serious head injury and was in critical condition. Mrs. Wilcox had suffered a broken right arm and a fractured collarbone. At the time the news article was written, the cause of the accident had not been determined.

He searched through several months of back issues of the paper but found no further mention of the accident. He took out his phone.

"Simpson Police Department," a woman's crisp voice answered his call.

"This is US Deputy Marshal Declan Owen," he said. "I'm looking into an incident in Simpson that happened more than twenty years ago. Do you have anyone who was working in the department who could answer a few questions for me?"

"What kind of incident?" the woman asked.

"A one-car accident in which a child was killed."

"Let me see what I can find. Can you hold?"

Declan was prepared to wait long minutes, but only seconds passed before a man came on the line. "Deputy Mashal Owen, this is Lieutenant Marco Carpenter. How can I help you?"

"I'm looking into one-car accident involving a woman named Jennifer Wilcox that happened twenty years ago."

"I know the case," Carpenter said. "I worked that accident. You remember the children, you know?"

"Do you know what happened? What caused the accident?" Declan held his breath, steeling himself for the answer.

"The mom was drunk, that's what happened."

All the breath went out of him, and it was a fraction of a second before he could speak. "I thought the little girl—the oldest one—distracted her while she was driving," he said.

"Maybe that's what the lady told people, but I was there. You could smell the alcohol on her breath. She had been picked up for public intoxication once before. I told the paramedics she needed a blood alcohol test, but between the woman's hysterics and the dead baby and injured girl, it got overlooked. By the time they tested her, she was below the limit."

"And the baby died when she was ejected from the car?"

"Mom hadn't buckled her into the child seat. We had ticketed her two weeks before the accident for failing to secure the baby. The little girl was old enough to buckle herself in, or she might have been killed, too, though she was pretty seriously hurt."

"What happened to the mother?"

"With no proof that she was over the legal

limit, nothing happened. She moved out of town before the girl was even out of the hospital. Why are you looking into this now, after so many years?"

He started to make up a story that would make it sound like he was looking into a case, but why bother? Sometimes the truth really was better. "I know the daughter," he said. "Grace Wilcox. She had questions about what really happened, so I told her I'd do some checking."

"Not a good story to have to tell her," Carpenter said.

"No, but sometimes it's good to have things cleared up."

He thanked Carpenter for the information, then ended the call and sat back. Grace had said her mother had started drinking heavily after the accident, but apparently it wasn't a new problem. Instead of admitting her own fault in the accident, she had blamed Grace. Maybe, after so many years of repeating the story, she even came to believe it.

Grace had to hear this. Never mind her feelings about him—she needed to know this. He started to call her, then changed his mind. This was news he needed to deliver in person.

He was pulling on his coat when his phone rang again. The screen showed an unfamiliar number from Denver. "Hello?" he answered.

"Declan Owen?" a woman's crisp voice asked.

"This is he."

"This is Victoria Green from the US Marshals Service in Denver, Human Resources. I'm sending you some documents you'll need to sign so that we can request a copy of your medical report related to your recent injury," she said. "I'll be emailing those. I need you to sign the forms electronically and send them back to me ASAP."

"Why do you need my medical records?" he asked.

"You're currently on medical leave due to a traumatic brain injury with resultant amnesia," she said. "That is correct, isn't it?" she asked.

"I was hit in the head, and I can't remember the events of a few hours," he said, cold creeping up his spine.

"A traumatic brain injury with resultant amnesia," she said. "The review board needs your medical records in order to determine if you are fit to return to duty."

"I'm going to return to duty as soon as a doctor releases me," he said. He hadn't thought much about when that might be. Right now, it suited him to remain in Eagle Mountain, close to both Terrence Barclay and Grace Wilcox.

"A review board will review your records

and decide whether or not you are physically and mentally capable of returning to your duties with the Marshals Service," Victoria said.

"Do I have any say in the matter?" he asked. "Do I need to secure an attorney?"

"This isn't a legal proceeding," she said. "It's an employment review."

"What happens if I don't sign the release form?" he asked.

"You won't be allowed to return to work."

He ended the call and sat, fuming. Ever since Barclay had escaped, Declan had feared for his job. He had thought by doing his best work and perhaps even by helping to recapture Barclay, he could redeem himself and once more excel at work he had loved. But as the weeks had passed, and especially since coming to Eagle Mountain, that possibility had felt more and more remote.

The general was going to come apart if he learned Declan had been kicked out of the Marshals Service. Declan would never hear the end of this, his biggest failure yet. Ironic, since law enforcement was the one thing he knew he had been good at. What was he going to do now? He could try to find a job with another agency, but that head injury was on his record now, and who was going to overlook that?

Terrence Barclay had a lot to answer for. He

would probably smile when he learned he had been responsible for the death of Declan's career.

THE TEXT ALERT on her phone roused Grace from the stupor she had fallen into. She was still on the floor with Bear, who hadn't moved, other than to lean against her comfortingly, occasionally licking tears from her face. She pulled the phone from her pocket and stared at a text from Search and Rescue. Car off-road at Dixon Pass.

Almost the exact message she had received the day Declan stumbled out of that blizzard and into her life. At least the weather was better today. And this accident didn't involve Declan, she reminded herself. She untangled herself from the dog and stood. The best thing she could do right now was to leave the cabin and help someone else.

"Come on, Bear," she said. "You go outside while I change." She let the dog out, then went to dress for a trek in the snow. A search and rescue call would keep her so busy for the next few hours that she wouldn't have time to think about her mess of a life.

DECLAN LEFT THE ALPINER, intending to head to Grace's cabin. But first, he had to stop for gas. As he pulled up to the pump, Arnie was coming out of the station. He spotted Declan and headed his way.

"Hey there," Arnie said. "Good to see you again. I didn't catch your name the other day."

"It's Declan. Declan Owen."

"You're the fed who's been staying at the Alpiner, right?"

Declan winced. Maybe to some people, a "fed" was anyone who worked for the US government. "I'm with the US Marshals Service, yes. How did you know?"

Arnie laughed. "You can't keep something like that quiet in a town this size," he said. "Stay here long enough and people will know your whole history. If you're like me and your two ex-wives also live in town, they'll know things about you that even you don't know."

"How is Mike doing?" Declan asked.

A shadow passed across the older man's expression. "He's okay."

"Is something wrong?" Declan asked.

Arnie shook his head. "Not really."

Was Arnie having doubts about his friend's son? "I guess Mickey is pretty grateful to you for taking in his son," he said. "Is he going to visit soon? I bet that'll be some reunion."

"Mickey's in Peru right now."

"I forgot. You mentioned that before. He's

probably even more relieved to know he's got someone in the state to help Mike."

"I guess so."

Doubt rang loud and clear in those three words, or at least it seemed to Declan. The hair on the back of his neck stood up. Call it cop sense or old-fashioned paranoia. Something wasn't right. "When was the last time you talked to Mickey?" he asked.

Arnie folded his arms across his barrel chest. "I haven't talked to him, actually."

"Why not?"

"Mike said he's impossible to get hold of down there."

"He doesn't have a cell phone?"

"Mike said where's he's working, they don't have good coverage."

Declan considered this. "When was the last time you talked to Mickey?" he asked, his voice gentle.

Arnie studied the ground between his boots. "About thirty years ago. To tell you the truth, we'd lost touch until Mike showed up."

"Have you talked to him at all since Mike came to live with you?"

Arnie shook his head, then looked up at Declan again. "Do you think I'm being conned?"

"You said Mike hadn't asked for anything, right?"

"No. And he's been a good worker. He's just…very secretive. Maybe that's just young people, but I'm worried he's in some kind of trouble, maybe with drugs or something. What do you think I should do?"

Declan wanted to tell the older man to run as far as he could from "Mike"—who might very well be a serial killer named Terrence Barclay. But Declan had zero proof of that assumption. If Mike was Barclay and Arnie confronted him, he might end up as Barclay's next victim. Barclay had avoided killing men thus far, but that didn't mean he wouldn't make an exception if he felt cornered.

"If I were you, I wouldn't do anything," Declan said. "See how things play out and let him come to you if he needs help."

Arnie nodded. "You're right. I'm probably worrying for nothing. Thanks for the advice. I need to get back to the store."

He left and Declan finished filling up the truck, but before he pulled away from the pump, he pulled out his phone and dialed Gage's number. "Where are you now?" he asked.

"I'm on my way back from Delta," Gage said. "Why?"

"I just spoke with Arnie Cowdrey. He's having doubts about Mike."

"What do you mean 'doubts'?"

"It turns out Arnie hadn't spoken to his friend Mickey in three decades before Mike turned up in his store. And he hasn't talked to him since, either. Arnie is beginning to wonder if Mickey is really in Peru, and why he can't be reached, even by cellphone."

"Yeah, that story did sound a little too convenient," Gage said. "But if he isn't Mickey's son, how did he know about Arnie in the first place?"

"You saw those pictures he has in the store, all neatly labeled with the names of the people in them. It sounded to me as if Arnie is happy to tell anyone the story behind those pictures. It was one of the high points of his life. It wouldn't have been that hard for someone clever to see the names on the photographs and feel Arnie out about his friend. He could have asked him when was the last time they spoke, did Arnie know where he was now and things like that. When he has all the information he needs, he breaks out this story of being Mickey's son."

"Arnie's too smart to fall for that."

"You and I both know smart people get taken in all the time."

"I'll admit, it's suspicious," Gage said. "But you don't have proof Mike isn't exactly who he says he is."

"Maybe you could stop him for a traffic violation and run his license," Declan said.

"He doesn't drive. He lives over the store and walks everywhere he needs to go."

"That fits Barclay's pattern, too," Declan said. "When he needs a car, he steals one, then abandons it." He rubbed the tight spot in the middle of his chest. "Mike could be Barclay."

"Or he could be exactly who he says he is."

"We can't take the chance of him being Barclay and killing again."

"All we can do is keep an eye on him. You know that."

He knew. No judge was going to give them a warrant to search Mike's rooms, and they had zero reason to detain him or surveil him. A force the size of the Rayford County Sheriff's Department didn't have the personnel for that kind of operation.

"I'm going to stick close and keep an eye on him," Declan said.

"You can't watch him twenty-four hours," Gage said. "And if he sees you, he can complain you're harassing him and I'd have to warn you off."

"He won't see me."

"He spotted you in Purgatory."

Declan grimaced. His history with Barclay

was riddled with screwups like that and had serious consequences. "That won't happen again."

"Keep me posted," Gage said.

Declan ended the call and pocketed his phone. His visit to Grace would have to wait. At least until he was more certain about who Mike Randolph really was and what he was up to.

Chapter Seventeen

Though the accident had occurred near the place where Declan's car had been found, this scene was very different. When Search and Rescue arrived, two sheriff's department vehicles and a highway patrol cruiser were already on site and had closed one lane of traffic to clear the way for rescue workers.

"Witnesses saw the car go over and called 911 right away," Deputy Shane Ellis told the group of rescuers. "The car is resting upside down about halfway down the slope. When I arrived on scene, I could hear someone shouting for help. A couple of cars had stopped and one guy tried to make it down to the car, but it's so steep and there's so much snow I don't think it's possible without climbing gear."

Grace stood with the others on the edge of the drop-off and stared down at a white car, wheels up and resting in a cluster of stubby pinion trees. The foliage obscured much of the vehicle, though the side nearest them looked smashed almost flat. How had anyone survived the crash?

"Eldon, I want you as incident commander," Sheri ordered. "Ryan and I will climb down and assess the situation. We'll do what we can to stabilize the vehicle. Carrie, you and Hannah get ready to rig a long line to bring up a litter. Grace, you assist them." She assigned volunteers to a handful of other jobs that needed to be seen to, then verified that Shane had already requested an ambulance.

Though Grace's heart was pounding as she listened carefully to Sheri's instructions, no one else seemed nervous. They all knew a person's life depended on them carrying out their jobs well, but everyone moved deliberately and calmly. All those hours of training kicked in. Even though she was relatively new to the group, Grace found she had already developed the muscle memory to correctly tie knots and to safely maneuver in the rough terrain.

"We're at the car," Sheri radioed up to the others a short while later. "The driver is alert and says he's uninjured. As soon as we stabilize the vehicle, we're going to try to get him out. He's hanging upside down, caught by his seat belt."

"Amazing what airbags and seat belts can do," Eldon said. "We're ready up top when you are."

While Hannah and Danny conferred on possible injuries to look for—given that adrenaline and fear could mask a lot in the first moments after an accident—the others milled around along the roadside, waiting for further instruction. Grace looked across the canyon, and the steep walls of red, purple and gray rock laced with ice. Sun sparkled on melting frost and felt warm on her face despite the below-freezing temperatures.

"All right, we have him out!" A cheer rose up at Sheri's message. "His name is Parker Overton. Looks like he's got some minor cuts from broken glass and some bruises from getting banged around. No broken bones, no open wounds. Yeah, he looks good. I don't think Danny and Hannah need to come down. Let's get the litter so we can transport him to the road. The medical folks can check him out there."

From that point, the rescue felt more like a training exercise. They sent an empty litter down on a line, and half an hour later it began the journey back to the top. "Coming up in that litter, practically vertical and wrapped up like a mummy, would frighten me almost as much as the trip down," Grace told Carrie.

"You and me both," Carrie said. She watched, hands on hips, as the litter inched up the line. "This looks and feels routine, but it's actually really dangerous. Of course, we won't tell Mr. Overton that."

Another cheer went up when the litter arrived at the top. Carrie and Grace undid the bindings securing Overton inside, then helped him to his feet. He was white-faced beneath his beard but managed a weak smile. "I don't ever want to do that again," he said.

"Here's hoping you don't." Shane stepped forward. "Can you tell me what happened?"

Overton grimaced. "I was paying too much attention to the gorgeous scenery and not enough to the road. I hit a patch of snow on the road and the back end of the car fishtailed a little, and the next thing I knew, I was flying." He wiped a hand across his face. "I thought I was dead." He turned to look back at the litter and the busy volunteers gathering up rope and other equipment. "Thank you all so much," he said.

Hannah and Danny insisted on checking out their patient but found no injuries beyond minor cuts and bruising. Overton declined a ride in the ambulance. Instead, Shane offered to take him home and help with arranging for what was left of his car to be hauled out of the canyon.

"I wish they all ended that well," Hannah said as they gathered their gear.

"That guy was really lucky," Grace said.

"His car's still stuck in the canyon," Danny

pointed out. "I wouldn't want to be the one paying to get it out."

"He probably wasn't worrying about his car when he was down there," Hannah said.

"Yeah, but I bet he is now."

Grace let the chatter wash over her as she helped clean and pack away gear. The sun was already sinking behind the mountains and there was a damp chill to the air that foretold snow. Sure enough, when she emerged from Search and Rescue headquarters at about four o'clock, light flakes began to fall.

Since Tommy had followed her home, she had fallen into the habit of watching for anyone following her. She chided herself for being silly—Tommy was harmless and he hadn't really done anything, had he?

She saw no one on the drive home, and by the time she parked her Jeep, the adrenaline of the afternoon had worn off, leaving her drained and chilled. She pulled on her helmet and started the snowmobile, anxious to take a hot shower, then sit in front of the fire with a cup of tea. She sped up the trail and stopped the snowmobile at the bottom of the cabin steps. Later she'd need to park it under the shed, but for now she only wanted to get inside and get warm.

As soon as she shut off the engine, Bear's frantic barking filled the air. He was inside the cabin, but when she turned to look, she could see him at the front window, barking and pawing at the frame. "What's wrong?" she called and mounted the stairs.

He howled, and his claws scrabbled on the wood floor as he raced to the door. As soon as she opened it, he ran out, past her and down the steps. Uneasy, Grace followed the dog to the corner of the house. He stood, back stiff, the hair at the base of his tail standing straight up, nose shoved into the snow beside a man's footprint.

Heart pounding, Grace looked around then. All was quiet, the snow smooth and undisturbed. "Who was here, boy?" she said softly. Bear looked up at her and whined, then trotted around the side of the house, following the tracks.

The footprints led all the way around the house. They were big prints, made with waffle-soled boots. They had to be a man's, and he had stopped at both back windows. To look in? To try to break in?

Back at the front of the house, she could see now that the tracks led away, toward the snowmobile trail to the road. The trespasser had walked up from that direction and returned the same way. She had been so focused on getting home that she hadn't even noticed the tracks before.

Grace shivered, her teeth chattering. She

hugged her upper arms and climbed the steps. "Come on, Bear," she said. "Come in."

The dog looked toward the trail, then turned and followed her into the cabin. She shut the door behind them and turned the dead bolt. Then she went up the stairs and retrieved her grandfather's shotgun. She checked that it was loaded, then carried it downstairs and set it beside the sofa. Bear would let her know if their visitor returned, and the shotgun would give her another layer of protection while she questioned the man. She realized she had become a cliché—the backwoods hermit who greeted visitors with a shotgun—but what else was she supposed to do? Calling the sheriff about a few footprints in the snow seemed excessive, especially since the falling snow would probably fill in the tracks before a deputy could get here.

She couldn't call Declan. Not after she had made such a big point of sending him away. She stoked up the fire, then sat, not on the sofa as she usually would, but in a chair she moved so that she was facing the front door. Then she waited. For what, she wasn't sure, but she didn't think she would be going to bed tonight. Just in case her unwanted visitor decided to return.

DECLAN, SLUMPED IN the front seat of the truck parked down the street from the natural foods store, watched as Arnie exited the store, crossed the street to a dirty white Subaru, got in and drove away. A few minutes later, Mike came out the front door. He locked the building behind him, then started walking, his steps taking him away from Declan.

Declan checked the time: 5:30. He gave Mike plenty of time to get a head start, then pulled out and followed. He was just in time to see Mike turn right on Main, so Declan went past the intersection, drove up and across one block and turned back toward Main. He parked and scanned the street and spotted Mike moving around the side of the bank.

Declan waited, but Mike didn't reappear. Had he cut across the back lot or gone into another door? Declan got out of the truck and walked quickly toward the bank. He approached cautiously, wanting to keep out of sight of his quarry. Shielded by a large lilac bush, he peered around the corner of the building and saw Mike standing in the drive-through. He passed a zippered bank bag to the teller and waited, talking. A few moments later the drawer in front of him popped open and he collected a slip of paper.

Declan turned to go back to his truck, then thought better of it. He waited until Mike walked back out on Main, then caught up with him. "Hey," Declan said.

Mike glanced at him. "Hey." He shoved both hands in his pockets and kept walking. Declan studied the side of his face. Nothing about him was familiar. "Is there something you want?" Mike asked.

"Arnie says you've been a big help to him."

Mike shrugged. "I do what I can. It's a lot, running a busy place like that by yourself."

"How did you end up in Eagle Mountain?" Declan asked.

"I like the mountains."

"And you remembered your dad had a friend here."

"I remembered after I came here. Dad said I should look him up."

"Who does he work for in Peru?"

Mike stopped and faced Declan. "What business is that of yours? Why are you asking so many questions?"

Declan took a step back, open hands at his sides, all innocence. "I'm just making conversation."

"Well, I don't feel like talking." He turned and strode down the street, back in the direction of the natural foods store.

Declan let him go. He walked back to his truck. He was getting in when a Rayford County sheriff's SUV pulled up alongside him. The window lowered. "How's it going?" Gage asked.

"About like you'd expect," Declan said. "Boring."

"So you haven't seen anything suspicious?"

"Mike just made a bank deposit. I assume that means Arnie has given him that responsibility. He'll have ready access to the money."

"Does Barclay care about that?" Gage asked. "I didn't read anything about him having stolen money in the past."

"There's nothing like that in his files," Declan said. "He doesn't even have any speeding tickets. He's as law-abiding as they come, except for murders and assaults."

"Right." Gage checked the street.

"I have a few hours I can spare you keeping an eye on him. You must have things you need to do."

He needed to see Grace. She deserved to know the truth about her accident. "You're sure?"

"Yeah." Gage held up a notebook. "I have reports to work on. I can't guarantee I won't get called for an emergency, but as long as I'm able, I'll babysit Mike for you."

"He lives above the store," Declan said. "He was walking that direction."

"I'll find him."

"Thanks." Declan turned the key in the ignition. "I should be gone only a couple of hours."

Gage drove away, and Declan pulled out. He drove toward Grace's, slowing as he reached the turn for the Forest Service road. He was just about to make the turn when a dark vehicle shot onto the highway, back end fishtailing as it made the sharp turn from the Forest Service road. Declan leaned on the horn while he waited for his breathing to return to normal. That guy had almost hit him. He looked over his shoulder, but all he could see was a pair of taillights disappearing over a hill.

He bumped the truck along the Forest Service road, knowing that if he tried to go much faster, the truck wouldn't stay in the ruts. Twenty-five minutes later, he parked beside Grace's Jeep, then turned the collar up on his parka and started the long trek up the snowmobile path.

Light glowed behind the drawn curtains on the cabin's front window, and Declan could hear Bear barking before he stepped into the clearing in front of the house. Grace's snowmobile was parked at the bottom of the front steps, her helmet on the seat. He felt the engine as he passed, but it was cold. He trudged toward the house and had his foot on the bottom step when the door eased open.

"Who's there?" Grace demanded. Or he thought it was Grace. Her voice sounded much harsher. Angrier.

He froze. "It's me, Declan," he said. When she didn't answer right away, he added, "I know you probably don't want to see me, but there's something really important I need to tell you."

The door opened wider, a triangle of golden light arcing across the porch. Then she stepped out, cradling a shotgun. "What are you doing here?" she asked, her voice more normal now. But she still hugged that gun like a lifeline.

"What's happened?" He wanted to go to her, but he didn't want to startle her. Not as nervous as she looked. "Why do you have that shotgun?"

Bear came out and sat behind her and regarded Declan with a grave expression. "Someone was here," she said and looked past him, into the darkness. "I came home and Bear was really upset, and there are footprints."

He took a few steps toward her now. "When was this?" he asked.

"I came home at about four-thirty or a quarter to five."

"You should have called me."

"I can't expect you to come running every time something spooks me."

"I'll be here for you anytime."

She moved past him, still cradling the gun. "You're here now. Look at this and tell me what you think."

He followed her as she pointed out the faint imprints from a man's boots. The snow was filling in the depressions, but there was still a faint outline visible here, a ridge of waffle sole there. The prints were clearer under the eaves, where the trespasser had walked up to look in the rear windows or maybe to test the locks. Declan crouched and took a few pictures with his cell phone, though he didn't know how well they would turn out.

"You say you saw these between four-thirty and five o'clock?" he asked. Almost two hours ago.

"Yes. They go all the way around the house, and then back into the woods alongside the snowmobile trail. I can't believe I didn't notice them when I rode in."

"I just walked that trail and I didn't see footprints," he said. Though it had been growing dark and he had been focused on staying to the narrow, packed trail.

"Maybe he walked in the woods, alongside the track," she said.

"Did you see anyone on the way in?" he asked.

"No, and the parking area was empty when I arrived."

"Just now, when I drove up, a car almost ran over me, coming from the Forest Service road onto the highway," he said. "Something big and dark-colored. Like a van."

"Bear was so upset," she said. "I think seeing him upset frightened me the most. He was frantic. You can see where he was scratching, trying to get out the door." She led the way back up the steps and into the cabin.

"Look." She pointed to fresh scratches and bite marks in the wood of the door and the frame. "He's never done that before," she said.

He pulled out his phone. "I'm going to call Gage."

"There's nothing he can do," she said.

"There might be."

Gage answered on the third ring. "Mike is in his apartment and hasn't moved," he said.

"I'm not calling about Mike," Declan said.

"What is it?" Gage was immediately all business.

"I'm at Grace's. She got home this afternoon and someone had been prowling around her cabin. I saw the footprints. She didn't see anyone or any vehicle, but when I was headed up here, a vehicle coming from this direction almost ran me off the road. I'm pretty sure it was a van. A van like the one Tommy Llewellyn drives."

"His van is broken down," Gage said.

"Maybe he had it repaired. I'm going to stay here in case he comes back. Can you put someone else on Mike Randolph and check out Llewellyn? I want to know where he was and what he was doing between four and six o'clock."

"I'll see what I can do, but we may have to

leave Mike on his own for a while. He may not even be the person we're looking for."

"All right," Declan agreed. The Marshals Service should have had a full team looking into Mike and following his movements. But Declan and maybe Gage were the only people who seemed to think he could be Terrence Barclay. "I just want to know if Llewellyn is harassing Grace after we warned him off."

"I'll see what I can find out," Gage said.

"I'll be here." He ended the call and turned to Grace. She had leaned the gun beside the door and stood facing him.

"If you need to go, I'll be all right," she said.

"I'm not leaving you."

She crossed her arms over her chest. "You don't owe me anything."

"No, but we need to talk."

"There's nothing to talk about. I've already explained—"

He touched her shoulder. "Just listen to me. Please? I learned some things today that you need to know."

Chapter Eighteen

Something in Declan's voice softened Grace's resolve. He didn't sound angry or hurt, more… excited. As if what he had to tell her was something good. Something she wanted to hear.

She moved to the sofa and sat. "All right," she said. "What is it?"

He sat at the other end of the sofa, and she was reminded of the first time he had sat here, naked and bleeding and confused. He had been imposing in spite of his vulnerability. She hadn't known then how gentle he could be or how complicated he would make her life.

"I called the police department in Simpson, Iowa," he began.

She stiffened. "Why did you do that?"

"I wanted to hear what really happened the day you were injured."

He wanted to confirm that her carelessness really had led to her sister's death.

"The story they told me wasn't the one you've heard all your life," he said.

"What do you mean?" Was it worse? Was there something else her mother hadn't told her?

"You didn't have anything to do with your sister's death," he said. "The officer I spoke to was at the accident that day. He said he could smell alcohol on your mother's breath. She had been arrested for public intoxication before. He asked for a blood alcohol test at the hospital, but the order got overlooked until it was too late. But he's certain she was impaired and that caused the accident."

"But my sister wasn't buckled in her car seat. Mom said I unbuckled Hope and distracted her."

"You didn't. The officer said your mother had been ticketed only two weeks before for not securing the baby in her car seat. He thinks she overlooked it that day, too. You were old enough to fasten your own seat belt—that's the reason you were protected that day."

Grace tried to make sense of his words, but they wouldn't sink in, floating on top of her consciousness. "But why would my mother tell me those things if they weren't true?"

"Because she didn't want to admit the accident was all her fault. You told me she started drinking heavily after the accident, but I think she was probably already struggling with alcohol when the accident occurred."

She squeezed her eyes shut, trying to look back and see her life as it had been then. But she couldn't. "I don't remember."

Declan took her hand. His skin was so warm, his voice so gentle. "It doesn't matter if you don't remember," he said. "Lieutenant Carpenter does. I can give you his name and number if you want to talk to him yourself."

"Maybe later." She leaned toward him. "Why did you do it? Why did you get in touch with the police?"

"Because I wanted to know the truth. Not what your mother told you, but the truth. It didn't make sense to me that you would have unbuckled your sister's car seat. Why would a child do such a thing?"

She swallowed and blinked past the prick of tears. She couldn't even decide how she felt—sad, hurt, angry.

"It's a lot to process," he said. "And maybe it would help to talk to a professional therapist about it. But for now, just know that you are not a bad person. You never were. What your mother did and said to you—that's part of her own illness, not on you. Can you believe that?"

"I want to try."

She sat for a long moment, head bowed,

her hand still clasped in his. After a while, he cleared his throat. "I had another interesting phone call," he said. "From the Marshals Service."

This was it. He had been called back to Denver. She tried to prepare herself for this news. "What did they want?" she asked.

"This was from the human resources department. They're going to be requesting my medical records for a review."

"They must be getting ready for you to return to work."

"I think it's more likely they're looking for a reason to let me go," he said.

She stared. He didn't look upset about this. "Why would they let you go?"

"The woman said they were concerned my head injury and subsequent amnesia would disqualify me from active duty."

"Oh no. What will you do?"

"I don't know. I know I'm good at my job and I can still do it. But it's been clear for a while that my supervisor doesn't want me around. I don't know what I'll do. Law enforcement is what I'm best at, I think."

"If they have to review your records, it sounds like you've got some time to decide."

"I do." He released her hand, his expression grim. "My dad is going to be furious."

She shifted, inching a little closer to him. "I'm not really one to give advice on relating to parents," she said, "but maybe, like my mom, he isn't seeing you as you really are."

"You mean I'm better than he thinks I am?"

"Something like that."

She moved closer, and he pulled her close and kissed her. It was the most natural thing in the world, and afterward they sat with their arms around each other, looking at the fire. Where was this going to lead? Grace didn't know, but she wouldn't waste time worrying. She had wasted too much time regretting a past that had apparently never happened. She wouldn't forfeit any chance at happiness, no matter how brief.

From his cruiser parked at the corner, Gage watched the rooms above the natural foods store. Flickering bluish light indicated the television was on, and infrequently a man's shadow moved across one window. Mike moving about. He seemed to have settled in for the night.

He pulled out his phone and hit the number for his wife. Maya answered on the second ring. "I'm going to be a little later than I thought," he said. "Something has come up."

"It's okay," she said. "Casey and I are going over to Sharon's place. Delia is coming, too, with her twins. The kids are going to play, and the moms are going to eat junk food and talk until we're hoarse."

He could hear the smile in her voice and pictured her playing with a strand of her blue-tipped hair as she talked. Everything about her was a little rounder with her pregnancy, and he was almost embarrassed to admit how much it turned him on. He would have laughed if someone had told him two years ago how much he would still be besotted with his wife.

"Sounds like an evening," he said.

She laughed. "You would hate it, but it's exactly what I need."

"Then have a good time."

"I will. And you be careful."

"Always."

With a last glance at Mike's apartment—nothing had changed—he put the SUV into gear and headed out to County Road 7. New snowfall hid the ruts in the road, and he had to slow even more to avoid being thrown about. He hit the high beams and hunched forward, watching for the turnout where Tommy Llewellyn's van had been parked. He braked as he drew alongside the place he was sure it had been, but the van wasn't there. The only indication that anyone had been there was a snow-free space the length and width of a van, and a fire ring of sooty stones. Had Tommy cleared out?

Gage drove farther, but the road began to narrow even more and he saw nowhere else with enough room to park a van. He had to go back a quarter mile before he found a place where he could turn the SUV around.

In town, he drove to the Ranch Motel. An older woman looked up as he entered, deep lines across her forehead getting deeper as she took in his uniform. "Can I help you, Deputy?" she asked.

"I'm looking for Tommy Llewellyn," Gage said. "I believe he works here."

"He gave his notice this morning," she said. "I told him he had to work two more weeks and give me time to find someone else for his position, but he said he had to move on."

"Did he say something had happened?" Gage asked. "A family emergency or something?"

"He just said it was time for him to be going." She waved her hand in the air. "I should have known better, hiring someone who lived in a van, but he seemed like a nice guy and I wanted to give him a chance. He was a good worker while he was here, anyway. Left everything in order."

"Did he leave a forwarding address or a place to send his final check?" Gage asked.

"No. He said I could donate whatever he was owed to a good cause." She wrinkled her nose. "That right there probably explains why he's still living in a van."

"Let me know if you hear from him." Gage handed her a card.

She read the card, then tucked it into a drawer beneath the front counter. "Has he done something wrong?"

"I just want to talk to him, that's all."

He left and returned to his SUV, but he didn't leave right away. He sat for a long time, thinking about Tommy, and about Mike, and about Terrence Barclay. Rootless young men who had all ended up in Eagle Mountain. At least, they were assuming Barclay was here. Gage sensed Declan's certainty about that, but was he making a mistake, believing the marshal?

What would Travis have done if he were here? As much as Gage wanted to prove that he was capable of running the sheriff's department by himself, he wouldn't have minded having his brother here to bounce ideas off of him. But Travis was apparently living up to his promise to his wife not to check in.

Gage put the SUV in gear and drove back downtown to the sheriff's department. Time to do a little more digging into Tommy Llewellyn, Mike Randolph, Terrence Barclay and Declan Owen.

DECLAN MADE PANCAKES for dinner, and they were as delicious as he had boasted. While they ate, Grace told him about the search and rescue call she had responded to that afternoon. "I can't believe how lucky that guy was," she said. "He went off the road into that canyon, and he walked away with only a few cuts and bruises. The other volunteers have all kinds of stories about people who have been killed or seriously hurt in similar accidents."

"Does it bother you, responding to traffic accidents, given your personal history?" he asked.

"I was afraid it would, but it doesn't," she said. "I guess because I don't remember my accident. And apparently what I thought I knew was wrong, anyway." Her voice broke and she set down her fork and stared at her plate. "I'm sorry," she whispered.

"Don't be." He leaned across the table and squeezed her hand. "It's been a big shock. I imagine it will take a while to process. But don't think you have to hide your feelings from me."

She nodded. "I'm used to hiding my feelings. I can't promise that will change."

"You don't have to change for me," he said. He cut a wedge from his stack of pancakes. "It doesn't work, trying to change for someone else, anyway. I tried it with my father for years and years."

"Do you think we ever get old enough for our parents to stop having so much influence on us?" she asked.

"I don't know. But I'm going to try to stop fighting the general so hard. I'm going to focus less on his opinion and more on what I think is right."

"That's a good idea." She picked up her fork again. She had been so preoccupied with his revelation about the real circumstances of her accident that she had almost forgotten about the stranger who had left those footprints around her cabin. "Do you think Tommy was back up here?" she asked.

Declan pushed his plate to one side and rested his elbows on the table, hands clasped. "I don't know," he said. "I didn't get a very good look at the vehicle that almost hit me at the intersection with the highway. It might not have been Tommy. And it might not have been coming from here."

"I didn't see any vehicles parked near the other trails along the road."

"Is there anywhere else he could have parked, to keep his van out of sight?"

"I don't know. Maybe. There are some private lots. Old mining claims. Someone could have pulled up in there, but it would be tough to do without getting stuck in the snow."

"Maybe he did get stuck and that's why he passed me two hours after you arrived home."

"I was wondering about that. I hate to think

he was here all the time I was in the house alone, watching and waiting."

He pushed back his chair and stood. "After we do the dishes, I'll make another check outside."

Grace stood at the front door while Declan made a circuit of the outside of the house. It was snowing harder now, big flakes dancing in the beam of the flashlight he shone into the woods around the cabin. "Should I put the snowmobile in the shed?" he asked.

She regarded the machine, already dusted with snow. "Leave it out," she said. "Just in case." In case one of them had to go for help quickly. She stared toward the trail to the road. She was probably worrying over nothing. Who would be out on a night like this?

DECLAN LAY AWAKE after they went to bed, Grace breathing evenly beside him. Was that Tommy's van he had seen? Why would he come back up here? Had Gage and Declan been wrong when they deemed him harmless? And what was Mike up to? Gage would have called if he had learned anything important about either man, but not knowing made Declan uneasy.

Bear growled, low and menacing. Declan was out of bed before his mind had fully registered the origin of the noise. By the time he had pulled on jeans and a sweater and shoved his feet into boots, the dog was barking and scratching at the front door.

"Don't let him out." Grace came into the living room behind him, her robe pulled around her. "I don't want him hurt."

"Is the shotgun the only weapon you have?" Declan asked.

"Yes."

He picked up the gun from beside the door and checked the load. Bird shot. He could hurt someone with this but not stop them. "Call 911," he said. "Tell them you've got a trespasser."

"You really think someone is out there?"

"I don't think Bear is upset over nothing."

"It will take forever for anyone to get here," she said.

"Call them, anyway."

"All right." She left the room and he turned back to the window. He couldn't see anything in the darkness. Bear had stopped barking but still paced the room, agitated.

Grace returned. She had dressed and was holding her phone. "I called. They said they would send someone, but it might be a while. I think there's only one officer on duty this time of night."

"I haven't seen or heard anyone moving

around," he said. "Maybe Bear's barking scared them off."

"I'll make some coffee." She started for the kitchen but took only a few steps before she froze.

"What is it?" Declan hurried to her side.

"I saw a light in the kitchen," she said, her voice low. "There shouldn't be a light."

He stared into the room, seeing nothing, then a flare of light, like the flame of a candle or a lighter or...

"I smell smoke," Grace said. She started toward the kitchen and he pulled her back as the small flare he had seen became a big one.

"The kitchen's on fire," he said. "We have to get out of here."

She grabbed Bear's collar and dragged him toward the door, where she snapped on his leash. They shrugged into their coats and stepped onto the porch.

The cold hit them like a slap, and sharp pellets of snow stung their cheeks. "Get on the snowmobile and go to your Jeep," Declan said. "You need to get out of here." He didn't think the fire was an accident, and he didn't want her around to face whoever had set the blaze.

She must have come to the same realization. "I can't leave you here with whoever this is," she said.

"I'll be fine." He took her by the shoulders and leaned close, wanting to make sure she could see his face. "I'm trained for this kind of thing," he said. "But I won't be as effective if I'm distracted by you. Go and get help."

She nodded and moved toward the snowmobile. She called for Bear, but the dog was already trotting around the corner of the house, nose to the ground. Declan racked the shotgun and headed after him.

Chapter Nineteen

Grace floundered through the deep snow to the snowmobile. She had forgotten her boots and had trouble finding purchase in her sheepskin slippers. She grabbed the helmet and shoved it on, then straddled the seat and fumbled for the key, her hands shaking with fear and cold. She didn't want to leave Declan and Bear, but going for help did seem the best way she could help.

The snowmobile's engine turned over, then died. She tried again. "Come on, come on," she chanted under her breath.

Then she was grabbed around the shoulders and flung to the ground. She screamed and tried to fight back, but a hard knee in her back drove her into the snow. She rolled over and tried to get up, but her attacker straddled her. She stared up at Tommy Llewellyn. At least, this man wore Tommy's orange knit hat, but he looked different. Harder and meaner.

"You're not going anywhere," he said. "Never again."

She screamed, and he hit her in the face, hard enough that her head snapped back and her vision blurred.

Frantic barking drew closer, and Grace struggled up to see Bear bounding toward them. "Bear, no!" she shouted.

Tommy turned away from her and the boom of a gun left her ears ringing. She tried to grapple with him, but he fought her off, and Bear bounded away.

"No!" The shout echoed around them. Tommy shifted his attention to somewhere behind her. She turned her head and saw the figure of a man stalking toward them through the snow. Declan was not naked this time, but the glow of the burning house patterned his body and face with patches of light and dark, like streaks of blood.

Tommy rose and dragged her up with him. "Drop the gun," he ordered.

Declan tossed the shotgun he had been carrying aside. Only then did Grace realize Tommy had the still-warm muzzle of a pistol pressed against her throat. She went very still, terrified to move, and stared at Declan, afraid of what he might or might not do.

"You're surprised to see me, aren't you?" Tommy asked. "I could tell you had no idea who I was. I heard that knock I gave you on your head did a number on your memory." He laughed, and Declan clenched his jaw to keep from roaring with outrage. He had to stay calm. To find a way to outmaneuver this killer.

"Hello, Terrence," he said. "Since I can't remember, why don't you tell me what happened that day?" He remembered the transcripts he had read of Barclay's interrogations, in which he talked about his crimes with what read like pride.

"Easy enough." Barclay shifted to tighten his hold on Grace. Declan forced himself not to look at her. He had to stay focused on Barclay. "I saw that woman on the side of the road, her arm in a sling, her tire flat," Barclay said. "I was the charming Good Samaritan, coming to her aid. I knew you were behind me. I stuck your gun—the one I took from you before— in her back and ordered her to flag you down. Then I hid behind her car while she did so. I knew you'd stop. You were crouched over her tire when I came up behind you and hit you in the head. Then I shot her. I stuffed her in your car, then stripped you and tipped you over into the canyon. The last time I saw you, you were sprawled on a ledge in the snow. I figure you'd freeze to death before you woke up, but I guess I was wrong about that. I drove the car I had stolen in Purgatory to a canyon I had passed a couple miles back, shoved it in, then walked the two miles back to where I'd left you. The weather was nasty, so nobody was around. They probably wouldn't have seen me in the snow, anyway. I took the woman's car and left. I ditched that car in some little town and found the van, parked behind a house that didn't look like anyone was in it. Then I drove back to Eagle Mountain and became Tommy Llewellyn."

"Who is Tommy Llewellyn?" Declan asked.

"A loser I met in jail the last time they picked me up. He said he was headed back home to Ohio or Michigan or wherever he was from as soon as they let him out. Easy enough to become him."

Grace made a choking noise, and Declan had to look at her. She had grown very still, but not passive. He could feel how alert she was. Waiting for a chance. The heat from the fire was intense enough that he could feel it here, fifty feet away. Grace had something in her hand. He realized it was the keys to the snowmobile, laced between her fingers.

Their eyes met. He blinked once, slowly, an acknowledgment that he knew what to do. Barclay was still going on about Tommy Llewellyn being such a loser when Declan groaned, clutched his chest and sank to his knees in the snow.

Barclay stopped talking. "What the—" He leaned toward Declan, loosening his grip just enough that Grace brought her hand up and stabbed the key right in his eye.

Barclay howled. He clutched at his face with his free hand. Grace grabbed for the gun in his other hand and it went off, firing into the snow, then they both lost hold of the weapon and it fell, disappearing beneath the snow. She jerked away from him and ran, not away and not toward Declan, but straight to the cabin.

"Grace, no!" Declan shouted, but she gave no indication that she heard. Barclay was already struggling back to his feet. Declan found the shotgun in the snow and used it like a club to hit Barclay in the head. Barclay dropped like a felled tree, landing facedown in the snow.

Declan pulled the laces from Barclay's own boots to tie his wrists and ankles, then he pulled off the boots and hurled them as far away as he could. Satisfied that the fugitive wouldn't be going anywhere, he ran after Grace.

More than half of the cabin was fully engulfed, choking smoke filling the rooms that had not been consumed. Declan pulled his jacket over his head, then plunged into what had been the living room and spotted Grace in the corner. She was clearing the shelves of her grandfather's notebooks, piling them onto a blanket she had spread on the floor.

"You have to get out of here!" he shouted over the crackling and popping of the fire.

She gathered the corners of the blanket and thrust the resulting bundle at him. "You take these," she said. "I'll get the rest." She picked up a second bundle he hadn't noticed before. "These are the ones I haven't transcribed yet."

"We have to get out of here," he said again.

"We will. But I'm taking these with me. This research is priceless." She hefted the bundle and turned, not to the door where Declan had entered, but to the window at the end of the house farthest from the fire. She shoved it up, knocked out the screen, then pitched the blanket full of notebooks into the snow. Declan did the same, then urged her out the window. He followed and they rested for a moment, on their knees in the snow, coughing out smoke and trying to catch their breath. "Bear!" she gasped. She struggled to her feet. "Bear!" she shouted.

The dog peered around the back of the woodshed. "Oh, Bear, it's okay." She beckoned and he crept toward her, then closed the gap between them and began licking her face.

She hugged the dog, and checked him all over. "I thought Barclay shot him," she told Declan. "But I guess he just scared him away."

Declan stood and helped her to her feet. "Where is Tommy?" she asked. "Or Terrence? Or whatever his name is?"

"He's tied up out front. I need to get back to him."

"I'm going to drag these farther away from the fire, then I'll join you."

Bear began barking again as Declan rounded the corner of the burning house, then he heard the roar of engines and a parade of snowmobiles pulled into the clearing, one after another. The lead snowmobile came to rest beside Terrence Barclay's prone body.

Gage cut the engine and lifted the visor on his helmet. "I heard the 911 call come in and figured you might need some help," he said. "But maybe I was wrong." He climbed off the snowmobile and met Declan beside Barclay. "What was Tommy Llewellyn doing up here?" he asked.

"Tommy Llewellyn is probably somewhere in Ohio or Michigan or whatever he's from and has no idea what's been going on here," Declan said. "Barclay says he met him in jail and decided to assume his identity during his time in Eagle Mountain."

Gage nudged Barclay with the toe of his boot, and the bound man moaned. "I guess he looks enough like that mug shot to fool most people," he said. He bent and grabbed Barclay's arm. "Come on."

Declan and Gage pulled Barclay to his feet. "Do you want to do the honors of taking him into custody?" Gage asked.

Declan shook his head. "I'm not officially on duty. You'd better do it."

While Gage read Barclay his rights and prepared to transport him back to Eagle Mountain, Declan joined Grace and Bear at the edge of the circle of light cast by the burning cabin. "I'm sorry about your home," he said.

"I'm sorry, too," she said. "But I'm glad we saved the notebooks. They were the most important things in there."

He put his arm around her. "Are you okay physically? Barclay didn't hurt you, did he?" His voice broke on the last words, the knowledge of how close she had come to death leaving him weak in the knees.

"I'm fine." She touched her cheek, where he could see a bruise forming. "He hit me, but I think I hurt him a lot worse."

He squeezed her more tightly against him. "You were amazing."

"I knew if I didn't do something, he'd kill me, and then he'd hurt you and Bear."

Gage joined them. "I'm sending Barclay to town with a couple of deputies," he said. "We'll stay until the fire is out and to gather what evidence we can. You two should get somewhere warm as soon as you can. I can have someone take you to Eagle Mountain."

"We'll take Grace's snowmobile and Jeep," Declan said. "I still have my room at the Alpiner. We can stay there."

"I'll want your statements as soon as possible," Gage said. "Tonight, preferably."

"We'll take care of it," Declan said.

"I have my grandfather's notebooks." Grace indicated the two blanket-wrapped bundles at her feet. "They need to be put somewhere dry as soon as possible."

"We'll see to that," Gage said. He clapped Declan on the back. "Good work," he said, then left to oversee the rest of the job.

Declan drove the snowmobile to Grace's Jeep, Bear loping along beside them. By the time they reached the Jeep, he and Grace were both shaking with cold. Fortunately, she kept the Jeep keys on the ring with those of the snowmobile, and the engine soon began pumping warmth into the cab.

Hannah Richards met them at the Alpiner and gave them hot chocolate and extra blankets. "You might as well take a hot shower and get into some dry clothes before you go to the sheriff's department," she said. "Jake already texted me that everyone is still up at the cabin." She patted Grace's shoulder. "I'm sorry about your home," she said. "But you can borrow some of my clothes. We're about the same size."

Declan thought he would never forget the details of that evening. He repeated the story so many times over the next few days, beginning with his statement at the sheriff's department that evening.

"You were right about Barclay being here," Gage said. "And everyone who wouldn't listen to you was wrong. That has to be a good feeling."

"Not really," Declan said. Grace had lost her home. He had almost lost her. He doubted this was going to endear him to his colleagues at the Marshals Service. He was relieved Barclay was in custody again but couldn't help wondering if he couldn't have done more to keep things from reaching this point.

It was almost morning when he and Grace finally returned to the Alpiner and crawled into bed, having to shove Bear over to make room for both of them.

She rested her head on his shoulder and sighed. "I guess we're even now," she said.

"Even?"

"I saved your life, and now you've saved mine."

"I didn't know we were keeping score."

"We aren't. But I like symmetry."

"You're a scientist," he said. "How often does nature come out even?"

She chuckled. "Almost never."

"You're wrong, anyway," he said. "You were the one who brought Barclay to his knees. All I did was overact and fake a heart attack."

"That was what really stopped him," she said. "You might have a career in melodrama." She snuggled closer. "I guess you'll just have to stick around and try to even things up again."

He started to ask her if that meant she wanted him to stick around, but he sensed she had already fallen asleep. It was a moot question, anyway. He had no intention of going anywhere.

DECLAN AND GRACE were drinking coffee and eating a late breakfast the next morning in the sunroom of the Alpiner when Gage stopped by. From the shadows under his eyes and the wrinkles in his uniform, Declan suspected the sergeant had not yet been to bed.

"I wanted to let you know Terrence Barclay is being transported to jail in Junction," Gage said. He moved to the buffet and helped himself to a cup of coffee, then came to sit across from Declan at the table.

"I hope you warned his escorts to never let down their guard," Declan said.

"I did. And I sent three people instead of two." He sipped his coffee and closed his eyes.

"You look exhausted," Grace said.

He opened his eyes again. "It's been a long night, but it was worth it. And your grandfather's notebooks are in the evidence vault at the station. You can have them whenever you're ready."

"Thank you," she said. "A lot of people are going to be really happy to know they're safe."

"Looks like you're getting all the loose ends tied up," Declan said. "And I guess we don't have to worry about Mike Randolph."

"His name isn't Mike Randolph," Gage said. "It's Gordon Keller. He left some time last night. After I left to check on Tommy." His eyes met Declan's. "I'm kicking myself for not doing more to find Tommy after I realized he wasn't at his campsite."

"By then he was probably already up at Grace's cabin," Declan said. "What's the story with Gordon Keller?"

"Arnie called the station this morning, pretty upset," Gage said. "Apparently the person he knew as Mike cleaned out the business bank account. About ten thousand dollars. He might have gotten away with more, except he didn't have access to Arnie's other accounts. His prints came back as a match for Keller, who has a history of pulling scams like this one. We've put out an APB, but it will take some luck to apprehend him."

"It always does," Declan said. "I'm sorry about Arnie. Keller wasn't Terrence Barclay, but he was up to no good."

"I notified the Marshals Service that we had Barclay in custody," Gage said. "And I made sure they knew you were the one who captured him. They didn't have much to say."

"I don't expect they did." Declan sipped his coffee. He had lived with this knowledge enough to feel philosophical. "They don't look very smart right now, insisting that Barclay wasn't in Eagle Mountain."

"Maybe this will help you keep your job," Gage said.

"Oh, I doubt that. I'm too much of an embarrassment." He set down his cup. "I was hoping maybe I could come work for you. I heard you need another deputy."

"We can't pay what the Marshals Service offers."

"I've got other incentives for staying here." He glanced at Grace, who smiled and looked down at her plate.

"I'll have to talk to the sheriff."

"He's your brother," Grace said. "Your recommendation ought to count for a lot."

"Provided I can come to terms with the idea of working with this guy on a regular basis." He nodded to Declan. "He does grow on you, though."

"He does," she agreed.

Gage drained his coffee, then stood. "We'll be in touch," he said. "I'm headed home to try to get some rest."

As soon as they were alone again, Grace turned to Declan. "Are you serious about staying in Eagle Mountain?"

"I am." He took her hand. "Do you think you could stand having me around?"

She turned her hand to twine her fingers with his. "Ever since that first day we met, I felt a connection to you."

"I'm amazed I didn't frighten you off, staggering out of the storm that way."

"It's not every day I invite a naked man into my cabin." She grinned. "I guess you could say I liked what I saw."

"You just love me for my body," he said.

She leaned closer. "I love you for your courage and your intelligence, and because you didn't give up on me, when I'd given up on myself," she said. "We joke about me saving your life, but you really did save mine when you went to the trouble to find out what really happened when I was a little girl. No one ever did anything like that for me before."

"Seeing you hurt made me hurt," he said. "I guess we're connected that way now."

"It's a little scary, but good, too," she said.

"It's very good," he said. "I never minded being alone before I met you."

"I thought it was the way I'd always live," she said. "Like my grandfather."

"You and your grandfather had each other," he pointed out.

"But not all the time, and not forever." She pressed her palm to the side of his face, and he caught the soft scent of floral lotion. "With you feels different."

"It feels like forever," he said. And sealed the pledge with a kiss.

* * * * *

Don't miss the continuation of
Cindi Myers's miniseries
Eagle Mountain: Critical Response when

Pursuit at Panther Point

goes on sale next month!

Get 3 FREE REWARDS!

We'll send you 2 FREE Books plus a FREE Mystery Gift.

FREE Value Over **$20**

Both the **Harlequin Intrigue®** and **Harlequin® Romantic Suspense** series feature compelling novels filled with heart-racing action-packed romance that will keep you on the edge of your seat.

YES! Please send me 2 FREE novels from the Harlequin Intrigue or Harlequin Romantic Suspense series and my FREE gift (gift is worth about $10 retail). After receiving them, if I don't wish to receive any more books, I can return the shipping statement marked "cancel." If I don't cancel, I will receive 6 brand-new Harlequin Intrigue Larger-Print books every month and be billed just $6.49 each in the U.S. or $6.99 each in Canada, a savings of at least 13% off the cover price, or 4 brand-new Harlequin Romantic Suspense books every month and be billed just $5.49 each in the U.S. or $6.24 each in Canada, a savings of at least 12% off the cover price. It's quite a bargain! Shipping and handling is just 50¢ per book in the U.S. and $1.25 per book in Canada.* I understand that accepting the 2 free books and gift places me under no obligation to buy anything. I can always return a shipment and cancel at any time by calling the number below. The free books and gift are mine to keep no matter what I decide.

Choose one: ☐ **Harlequin Intrigue Larger-Print**
(199/399 BPA GRMX)

☐ **Harlequin Romantic Suspense**
(240/340 BPA GRMX)

☐ **Or Try Both!**
(199/399 & 240/340 BPA GRQD)

Name (please print)

Address   Apt. #

City   State/Province   Zip/Postal Code

Email: Please check this box ☐ if you would like to receive newsletters and promotional emails from Harlequin Enterprises ULC and its affiliates. You can unsubscribe anytime.

Mail to the **Harlequin Reader Service:**
IN U.S.A.: P.O. Box 1341, Buffalo, NY 14240-8531
IN CANADA: P.O. Box 603, Fort Erie, Ontario L2A 5X3

Want to try 2 free books from another series! Call 1-800-873-8635 or visit www.ReaderService.com.

---

*Terms and prices subject to change without notice. Prices do not include sales taxes, which will be charged (if applicable) based on your state or country of residence. Canadian residents will be charged applicable taxes. Offer not valid in Quebec. This offer is limited to one order per household. Books received may not be as shown. Not valid for current subscribers to the Harlequin Intrigue or Harlequin Romantic Suspense series. All orders subject to approval. Credit or debit balances in a customer's account(s) may be offset by any other outstanding balance owed by or to the customer. Please allow 4 to 6 weeks for delivery. Offer available while quantities last.

Your Privacy—Your information is being collected by Harlequin Enterprises ULC, operating as Harlequin Reader Service. For a complete summary of the information we collect, how we use this information and to whom it is disclosed, please visit our privacy notice located at corporate.harlequin.com/privacy-notice. From time to time we may also exchange your personal information with reputable third parties. If you wish to opt out of this sharing of your personal information, please visit readerservice.com/consumerschoice or call 1-800-873-8635. **Notice to California Residents**—Under California law, you have specific rights to control and access your data. For more information on these rights and how to exercise them, visit corporate.harlequin.com/california-privacy.

HIHRS23

Get 3 FREE REWARDS!

We'll send you 2 FREE Books plus a FREE Mystery Gift.

FREE Value Over $20

Both the **Harlequin® Desire** and **Harlequin Presents®** series feature compelling novels filled with passion, sensuality and intriguing scandals.

Get 3 FREE REWARDS!

We'll send you 2 FREE Books plus a FREE Mystery Gift.

FREE
Value Over
$20

Both the **Romance** and **Suspense** collections feature compelling novels written by many of today's bestselling authors.

THE NORA ROBERTS COLLECTION

40% OFF!

Get to the heart of happily-ever-after in these Nora Roberts classics! Immerse yourself in the beauty of love by picking up this incredible collection written by, legendary author, Nora Roberts!